Figures in the Landscape

Vashti Farrer

Figures in the Landscape

Acknowledgements

'Letter in a Strange Hand', Shortlisted, My Brother Jack Short Story Award;
2nd, Society of Women Writers Short Story Competition, December 2004
'Strays', 3rd, FAW Mona Brand Competition
'Special Wording', Commended National Short Story Competition,
University of Canberra, 2002; Winner, Society of Women Writers Short
Story Competition, December 2004
'All Round the Room', *The Outback*, Vol. 2, 2017
'Had As Leif Control', *backstory Journal* 2 (Swinburne University), September
2016 http://www.backstoryjournal.com.au/category/issues/issue-two
'Love Bytes', *Australian Book Review*, July 1992, No. 142;
Microstories, Angus and Robertson, 1993
'Quail', *Southerly*, Vol. 52, No. 4, December 1992
'Mr Brown Goes Out', *backstory journal* 6 (Swinburne University)
http://www.backstoryjournal.com.au/category/issues/issue-six
'The People on the Bus Go Up and Down', *Glass Walls: Stories of Tolerance
and Intolerance from the Indian Subcontinent and Australia*, 2019
'A Handcart in the Street', *The Age Monthly Review*, Vol. 4, No. 3, July 1984
'One Plain, One Purl, Two Sugars', *Southerly*, Vol. 59, No. 1, Autumn 1999;
Shortlisted, University of Canberra National Short Story Competition 1997;
5UV Adelaide, 3 July 1999

Figures in the Landscape
ISBN 978 1 76109 125 4
Copyright © Vashti Farrer 2021
Cover image: Mitchell Library, State Library of New South Wales
[PXE 921 (v.2), FL9160116], used with permission

First published 2021 by
GINNINDERRA PRESS
PO Box 3461 Port Adelaide 5015
www.ginninderrapress.com.au

Contents

There, But For the Grace...

The Rocks, New Year's Day, 1900

Mildred Burke, landlady: On Sunday morning early, me and Bill went down to Circular Quay to see the ships in dock. Crews were up the rigging furling sails, but they'd get leave to go uptown for New Year's, to see the sights. We can hear the noise from Windmill Street.

We've been here ever since we got married and know everyone. Our George used to play with kids in the street and we'd keep an eye on each others'. Now most of them are grown. George is twenty-one, working for a carpenter over Glebe way and walking out with Annie French, live-in help for the Paines that live down Ferry Lane. But Sunday's her day off, so they planned to join the fun and quite right, I told them, only they come round for Sunday dinner first; rabbit pie with gravy, mashed potato and peas then rice pudding, with a nice cup of tea to wash it down.

On Monday, New Year's Day, they said how lads marched up and down George and Pitt Streets blowing trumpets and twirling rattles loud enough to scare the dead till midnight then everything went quiet, and folks headed home to bed.

But I had a feeling this year would be different, New Year's Eve being Sunday and they don't like you celebrating Sundays.

Then two weeks later, the papers said plague had broken out in Adelaide, when I thought we were rid of it. The first the public knew was Adelaide Hospital closed its doors and police were stopping anyone getting in or out.

Dr Ramsay Smith, President Central Board of Health, Adelaide, Monday, 15 January: We'd been warned Australia could be visited by plague, but warnings had gone largely unheeded because of our remote position. However, in mid-November when the *Formosa*, from Noumea berthed, she was placed under quarantine because of appalling conditions. On 1 January, an eighteen-year-old German sailor, Eppstein from *Formosa*, who'd jumped ship heading for Gawler six weeks before, was brought into Adelaide Hospital, semi-delirious, claiming he'd been lying under a tree for two weeks without food. His repulsive swag and clothing were burned, but his medical condition was not diagnosed initially as plague. Other diseases were considered. However, once doctors were certain it was plague, Eppstein was isolated in a shed outside the hospital buildings and from then on carefully watched. I regret to say he died last Friday afternoon and a post-mortem confirmed it was *Pestis Bubonica Haemorrhica*, a most dangerous form of plague, mainly confined to the internal organs.

Soon after, a nine-year-old boy, Philip McCann, also from Gawler, was admitted and duly isolated and I took immediate precautions – no patients were to be discharged within ten days and the number of admissions was to be restricted. Any changes in symptoms or the development of new diseases in patients or staff were to be reported immediately to doctors treating them and all communication with the wider community was limited solely to the delivery of food and drink.

Bill Burke, husband of Mildred, casual labourer: I was laid off down the docks a while ago on account of a bad back so can't lift anything too heavy, but I take a day's labouring on the wharves when I can get it because every little helps.

Our terrace is not big but once George moved out, I re-plastered his room a nice pale blue and added a fancy stencil round the walls and Mildred added new curtains and her best washbowl and jug and we let it out. We've a nice, quiet gent from Melbourne with us and it's working out well.

Mildred's been on about plague, but I told her Adelaide's a long way from Sydney, so we'll be fine. It started fifty years ago in China and has been moving round the world ever since. Sixteen have died in Noumea, but that's a thousand miles from Sydney and any ships from there will be quarantined.

Dr Ramsay Smith: Eppstein was buried with strict instructions, the body moved under supervision of an inspector from Central Board. It was wrapped in a blanket soaked in disinfectant, then put inside a waterproof covering and placed in a coffin with more disinfectant. The coffin was enclosed in an oblong box again with disinfectant and taken by cart to Largs Pier, to avoid going through Port Adelaide. Once on a boat, it was towed to Torrens Island and buried in a grave seven feet six inches down to groundwater and the cart and boat thoroughly disinfected.

Mildred Burke: Bill had *almost* convinced me there wasn't a danger to Sydney when a big pile of dead rats was found on Huddart Parker Wharf not far from us. Then I remembered dead rats were found round Gawler too. These were off the *Maroc* from Noumea. Rats don't take notice of quarantine. They head for the nearest warm drains.

Dr John Ashburton Thompson, President, Board of Health, & Chief Medical Adviser to Government of NSW: It's thought likely the plague bacillus enters the skin through a flea bite, or abrasions with flea or rat faeces. Incubation is from two to six days, followed by fever, malaise, pain and swelling in lymph nodes, armpits, groin and the neck.

We currently have three hundred doses of Haffkine's prohyylactic from last year and I've ordered a further ten thousand doses to be sent from overseas. In the event of an outbreak or epidemic, all medical staff and those who come into contact with victims will be inoculated.

Mildred Burke: Then on 19 January, Arthur Paine, Annie's boss, come down with it. He's a carter on Central Wharf and came home feeling crook with stomach pains and took a dose of castor oil, then vomited and passed out. Next thing, the whole household's being sent to quarantine. That's Arthur, his missus, their two little girls, his sister Hannah and Annie. She's only sixteen but her family's in the country and she barely had time to scribble a note saying they was off. After that, no one was allowed down Ferry Lane. The street's too narrow for barricades round houses, so they sealed it off both ends.

Bill Burke: There's a rumour going round, timber houses'll be burnt to stop it spreading, but Paine's house is brick, so it'll stay. Most houses round here are cramped with shoddy add-ons, climbing the hillsides. Some streets so narrow the drains don't work and the privies smell. You can hardly see where one backyard ends, and another starts.

Annie French, servant: When Mr Paine come home sick, we was all worried. He were in terrible pain and during the night turned delirious. I don't know where he got it. The house is a two-up two-down with top drawing room or attic where I sleep, and a basement not used for nothing but storage. They say to look out for rats but they're all down Ferry Lane, drains and cesspits and out back near the rubbish tip. At night they're skittering in the ceiling and sounds like there's hundreds and I'm scared one'll drop on me face and start gnawing.

There's a policeman outside now. No one's allowed in or out. We're to wait for the ambulance but can only take one bundle each. Me and Mrs Paine raced round packing and the girls insist on taking their new dollies they had for Christmas.

Dr Ashburton Thompson: I've written to Dr Ramsay Smith at Royal Adelaide Hospital saying I thought it prudent to isolate a wharf labourer at quarantine for observation. I regret to say proofs by culture and inoculation furnished by Dr Frank Tidswell, my bacteriologist, are complete and the disease is definitely plague. I have no doubt the patient was inoculated by a flea, of which there is visible evidence, but his case is extremely mild, and it may be no other human beings are infected. The epidemiological enquiry is being actively prosecuted, but clinical and bacteriological account will be forwarded as soon as possible. Meanwhile, the household has been isolated with the patient, and the house closed.

Jimmy Higgins, local urchin: The Paines got took away today and their house sealed off. I asked the copper if they was going to die but he said, Gawn, get out of it. Clear orf! So I bolted but come back to watch the men carry their stuff up the steps from Ferry Lane. Took them more'n an hour to load up mattresses, kapok, straw, a baby's cot, pillows, blankets, shawls and dead cats. Then the cart come up Windmill Street, only Mr Burke said it weren't going to quarantine but to a 'cinerator for burnin'. Cats too.

I give his missus a note from Annie and she give me a penny. I didn't ask. She just did. I'm known round here for doing jobs. They knows I'm good as and I usually gets a penny. And most days I find stuff like pencils and screwdrivers, scissors, spanners even. I look down as I'm walkin' and sometimes it's things people have lost and if I finds the owner, he sometimes gives me sixpence. Trouble is Ma's always wanting me to mind me little sister Rosie, so she can get on with washing. Rosie's a bit too keen on the mangle and Ma's scared she'll crush her fingers. But it means Rosie's hanging round all day whinin' like a mozzy in me ear. What's this for, Jimmy? What you want that for? and soon as we pass the grocers on the corner it's Can I have some aniseed cats, Jimmy? and I tell her girls as don't say please and ta gets nothin'. But I usually gets her a couple anyway and a humbug for meself.

Dr Ashburton Thompson: Despite my recommendation that the Coast Hospital be used in the event of a major outbreak, the government has insisted all plague cases be sent instead to the Quarantine Station at North Head despite there being a limited forty-eight-bed hospital on site and accommodation only for three hundred non-infected contacts. The Coast Hospital is the obvious place as it's properly set up for such an emergency but the government feels it would be dangerous to move patients presently at the hospital and when this is all over it may be necessary to destroy hospital buildings because of the risk of continuing infection and this would of course involve considerable extra expense.

The first thing, however, that must be done is to kill the rats. I say this without hesitation while still acknowledging the importance of removing the filth that attracts them, but from the outset we must concentrate on killing rats.

Mildred Burke: Everywhere you go you hear people talking plague and what starts it. Some say mosquitoes, others it's handling dirty paper money from people's pockets but there's some thinks it's bad air and we should burn barrels of pitch in the streets. Now they're saying it's fleas! I'd have thought they was too tiny, but it seems they give it to the rats and when the rats die the fleas hop onto humans!

Dr Ashburton-Thompson: I know of no worse place for filth than some parts of Sydney, not even the London slums of which I've had experience. Conditions in some areas are appalling, nothing but a collection of filthy brick huts, I cannot call them houses, and other such places unfit for human habitation, not to mention the very real threat of open sewers.

It's not uncommon to find houses with three rooms leading one into the other and the middle room sometimes with no window at all or, if one exists, the light is shut off by the walls of neighbouring houses. Every room, including the kitchen, doubles as a bedroom, and whole streets of small houses have no conveniences at all. Add to this damp, arising from there being no damp courses or else poor roofing and guttering, and the situation is dire.

Annie French: Mr Paine got took off by ambulance. He looked real bad on the stretcher, grey as the blanket they threw over him. We went by horse and cart and the neighbours stood at their doors to see us off. George's ma waved, so she got my note. The horses took us down to Cowper's Wharf at Woolloomooloo, and I didn't feel nervous till I saw the little green ferry with its black funnel. They call 'em Death Boats and my old gran says if you takes a trip in them, you don't come back, and you can't miss their woo-hoot. Scares me whenever I hear it and it don't fool me the names they give them, like *Rose* and *Dayspring*. They're still death boats. Ours was *Lorna Doone* and all the way over to North Head I kept thinkin' maybe it was *Lorna Doom* and I'm having to pretend for the kiddies' sakes. Isn't this fun on a boat, but they say nothin' and sit starin' ahead.

Dr Ashburton Thompson: I've taken the precaution of arranging for eighteen specially trained nurses from the Coast Hospital to take up residence at the Quarantine Station for as long as necessary. They'll be under the supervision of Head Nurse Ford. As well, there'll be four ambulance drivers, extra cooks, laundresses and others.

Mrs Paine: I told them he'd been down A.U.S.N. wharf ten days ago carting bales of wool to Central Wharf. Maybe that's where he got it. He said he felt giddy and got a headache driving through Pitt Street but made it home. Only now they're saying all our friends and everyone has been in contact has to go to quarantine too. So my mother Mrs Holms, and Arthur's brother Harry, and our friend Mrs Smith, who lives at 67 Lower Fort Street. They're not saying they have it, mind, but it's best to be sure, so they all have to stay at North Head for ten days.

Word of Arthur being sick spread like measles. Most people didn't come to the house, but I could still see them up the top of Ferry Lane and knew they was talking about us. And even when he was lying there waiting for the ambulance, we got a visit from Missionary Mathers. Ma goes to his services and must have said something. The policeman stopped him coming in, but he still knocks on the door wanting to speak to Arthur. I told him, You can't. Arthur's got plague and a problem with his heart. Only that don't stop Mathers natterin'. So I said Arthur's a good man but a peculiar one and he's not too fussed about preaching, and Mathers says, Has he been saved? The cheek of it! I said, I've got a husband with plague and for all I know might die any minute and I'll be left a widow with two kiddies to support and there's you on the doorstep waiting for his soul. I know it's his job, but it was a bit much, considering.

Bill Burke: I went down the docks a while back lookin' for work and was told a ship were in needed cleaning bad, only they warn us we'd need a nip of rum before we started. Well, it turned out the smell was so bad in the hold we needed several. She'd been stuck out at sea for weeks on end while her cargo rotted and rats took over. I didn't have time to tell Mildred and anyway she'd have tried to stop me. Truth is, I weren't too keen meself, only the pay was good, and I planned to surprise her with a tin of corned beef for tea that night. Our orders were to clean her out like we would for cholera; fresh and bilge water tossed overboard, and all bedding and clothing sent for quarantine launderin' and mail fumigated. But soon as they open the hatches, hundreds and hundreds of rats poured onto the wharf like a black wave. Ropes and baffles didn't stop 'em teeming over each other to keep going. It give me shivers just watchin' as they headed up the hill towards Pottinger Street.

Mildred Burke: We've always had stray cats round. They look after theirselves and don't cause bother except with howling or fighting. Poor things are flat out now. One turned up this morning, a rat stickin' out his mouth like a big moustache and I started to laugh till I realised it were his gift. He planned to move in. I screamed and Bill come and grabs the rat by the tail and throws it in the 'cinerator down the bottom of the yard. Then I find the blighter's already been at me mutton fat soap in the wash house. Now we got a cat. Tibbles.

Plague can kill you if you come down with fever and shakes and get big black lumps under your arms, so I can't understand how Bill can stay so calm. All he says is, It's different this time. They won't be painting red crosses on doors and calling, Bring out yer dead, and every night he's there snoring away while I'm still tossing and turning.

Bill Burke: Of course, it's not just disease you got to worry about with rats. It's damage done to cargoes. They go for anything edible like wheat and vegetables, fruit, even hay. Shipping companies have to treat cargoes with sulphur dioxide and cyanogen to stop 'em. Otherwise they'd lose thousands of pounds' worth.

Jimmy Higgins: The day Paines' stuff went, Mr Han were there with his cart of fruit and veg. Some kids round here call him Chink or Chinaman and say you don't want to touch coins that's been in his pockets. But that ain't fair. He's a good bloke. Lets me pat his horse and sometimes gives me an apple with only a bit of bruise or maybe a spotty ripe banana like. Rosie too if she's with me.

Mr Ah Han, Chinese vegetable seller: Last time smallpox come, my father say our people blamed. Dragged off middle of night. Nobody buy fruit, so business bad. Now plague come, I worry for my family.

Mrs Paine: No sooner did we reach North Head than an ambulance backed down to the wharf and took Arthur off to hospital. I didn't even get to say goodbye and started to cry when I saw it rumbling off through the trees, but Hannah held my arm and nodded towards the girls so as not to upset them. We were waiting on the wharf for ages, but Annie played with them All I could think of was Arthur, that I might never see him again.

We were told we'd be staying in a building up the hill and I'm thinking we'd have to lug our bundles all the way up when a couple of men came onto the wharf and took them. Then one grabs the girls' dollies and they're sobbing and Annie's saying the dollies are only going for cleaning, but it takes all three of us to calm them.

Annie French: Once the clothes was gone, we was left waitin' till two nurses come down and says to follow 'em to the showers, only I've never had a shower. I've always been a bit nervous of water on me head on account of I can't swim. I top and tail each day and bath on Sunday, that's hair-wash night when the tub comes out and water's boiled and we take turns, littlest first then goin' up in size with me last usually, being the servant, only sometimes Mr Paine lets me have my turn afore him on account of he gets dirtier down the docks than I do in the kitchen.

Mrs Paine: Inside it's cool and dim with metal walls round showers higher than our heads. It's one shower each with the girls in together. The nurses tell us to take everything off, stays, drawers, the lot, and leave them outside, then we has to step down in this tub in the floor. That's when I see the eye slot in the door and know they're spying on us like in gaol and the girls start crying 'cos they don't know the woman washing their hair and they're scared and hate having their hair washed anyway. Then suddenly the water comes out burny hot and stinging and the girls are screaming and one nurse yells at them not to be cry-babies, while the other's shouting, It's only phenol. But that's carbolic, no wonder it stings like the devil.

Annie French: We come out raw red and the girls won't stop crying and I don't blame 'em neither. But the nurses give us towels and clean clothes while ours is fumigatin'. Nothing fits, but enough for now and I can see through another doorway the big boilers where our things is being steamed and know everything'll shrink and the colours run most likely.

Mrs Paine: They won't tell us anything about Arthur even though I keep asking. All the nurses'll say is, Well as expected and Not to worry, but I do, him lying there all by himself in the hospital.

Head Nurse Ford, Quarantine Station: Being a quarantine hospital, there are more rules. Staff going on shift are required to change out of their clothes and shower at one end of the ward then put on uniforms. When they finish, they do it again in reverse. We currently have extra staff in residence, but the station is not designed to take such numbers, so some nurses are being accommodated in tents for the duration.

For contacts not infected with plague, there are separate wooden accommodation blocks. Dormitories for men and women, with married couples split up, but boys under two allowed to stay with their mothers since putting them in a ward with total strangers would be upsetting.

Hospital wards are painted pale green, which is considered soothing for febrile patients. We provide mosquito netting for each bed as they're bad on the station and put up sheets between beds in infectious wards, for privacy. Currently, beds are widely spaced with plenty of room between for big vases of eucalyptus leaves, which give a pleasant fragrance, but if more cases develop and extra room is required, beds can easily be moved closer together.

As a general rule, we insist on disinfecting everything that comes on site with phenol, but the most important rule is not allowing contact between patients and others.

Mrs Paine: The food's good and there's enough of it and for once I don't have to cook. But after that first dinner there was a great to-do when a nurse come to give us our needles. Everyone that's been a contact has to be inoculated, but the girls didn't understand and cried and squirmed and wriggled and we had to hold them still for long enough.

Annie French: In Ferry Lane, I did the laundry, so I worried about the clothes. They come back with some still damp, others shrunk too small to wear again. But worse still, the girls' dollies are ruined. They're only cloth with painted faces but the bodies are hard and lumpy, the faces run so they look like clowns. The girls are heartbroken and won't play with them.

That first night were hard. Strange beds in a strange place and it took ages to settle the kiddies, but next day was brighter once we got out after breakfast. Mrs Paine asked to go up to the hospital but weren't allowed. Still, the girls play hide-and-seek and they're happy.

Bill Burke: It's a losing battle. I keep putting down traps and baits every day, but nothing stops them. Catch one rat and five take his place. I borrowed a terrier for a week to get on top of them but even he couldn't manage and by week's end I had to give him back. I've written to the council, but they must get hundreds of letters and can't cope.

This morning, I found they've made tunnels under the backyard and kitchen floor and they're gettin' so bold they're climbing the stairs to the bedrooms. I've put big tins of water under the bed legs or Mildred would never get to sleep. Otherwise notices are going up:

Plague is present in Sydney.
It has been introduced by diseased rats and is in danger of spreading.
Anyone finding sick or dead rats is to tell the Board of Health straight away.

Mrs Paine: Hannah and I were stuck at North Head doing nothing. They wouldn't let me see Arthur, so we sat outside most days, only going indoors for meals. But I asked for Annie to be given work.

Annie French: They put me on sewing shrouds, which I hated. Not that there's much sewing to them but watching 'em pile up gave me the creeps like waiting for people to die.

And after our showers, my skin's started to peel off in strips.

Bill Burke: There are people trying to make money from others being scared. Adverts for cures or ward-offs. Vitatadio's a herbal remedy from Tasmania supposed to cure everything from cancer to consumption. And others, probably more gin than anything, but what good would any do you once you got carted off to North Head?

Mr Ah Han come round today and says there's posters going up in Chinese round the markets warning about plague and rats, but he says it's hopeless where his rellies live. They try to keep their houses clean, but landlords won't pay for repairs, so houses get more and more run-down.

Mildred Burke: I can't believe it's the end of January already. The Paines are back home now. The family didn't catch it and Arthur only got it mild, so he'll be home in a couple of days. But for a welcome, I made a big pot of stew and left a jug of milk and loaf of bread for the kiddies.

Mrs Paine: The stairs were hosed down and fences limewashed and inside the house was almost new. Out in the yard, the rubbish tip's gone and the cesspit filled in and they'll be fitting us with proper toilet to the sewer. Some furniture's here still, but we'll need new mattresses and blankets.

Mildred Burke: The papers haven't reported any new cases, but police have been round telling everyone that's been in contact with Paines has to go to North Head. When the constable knocked on our door, we had to tell him about George and Annie, not that he's seen much of her since New Year's he's been that busy. But they said, Don't worry about him, only we was to pack a bag each and report to Woolloomooloo wharf. We'd have asked our gentleman lodger to look after the place since he's not met George or Annie, but he's upped and off to Melbourne. Family reasons but if you ask me, he was scared and scarpered.

Bill Burke: The men Arthur works with down the docks are off to quarantine so are his neighbours in Ferry Lane. Mr Ah Han and his wife and kids live in Queen Street but his parents are in Wexford Street near Belmore Markets and since Mrs Paine bought vegies from him, he and his family are off to North Head too.

Arthur Paine: It's good to be back home. Thought I was a goner there for a bit. Didn't know where I was or what were wrong with me and the pain were so bad, I felt sure I was on the way out. Feel limp as a wet rag still, but that'll pass they say, so I'll be able to work back at Central Wharf soon as they'll have me.

Mildred Burke: We didn't bother lockin' up 'cos they had to get in to fumigate. I looked for Tibbles everywhere but couldn't find him, so I hope he's all right. There's plenty of rats, so he won't go hungry, and I left a big bowl of water in the yard.

Mr Ah Han: My wife very frightened. But Mister Burke and Missy Burke on ferry too. He say not to worry.

Bill Burke: It was just over a week and it weren't too bad. A bit of a break for us. But it got my goat how people were treated different. We were in a building with room to move but Mr Ah Han and his wife and kids were in a small tent. The doctors and nurses didn't seem to think it unfair and Mr Ah Han never complained, but still. We've not seen him since we come back but houses in Queen Street have gone so I s'pect he's gone to Wexford Street.

Our house weren't pulled down but they're still cleaning round here, so we can't move back in yet. At least the rats have mostly gone, along with the stencil that took me so long. The rooms have been washed down with carbolic and the colour's bleached, but it'll give me something to do getting it looking nice again for another lodger. That's if we can find one prepared to move into The Rocks.

Mildred Burke: I'm sad about Tibbles. We hadn't had him all that long but he'd fitted in. The noise of clean-up must have scared him

We've starting to see names in the papers. John Makins worked for a steamship company in Sussex Street and developed a lump under his arm and stomach pains with high fever and delirious. There's boarding houses along Sussex Street and underground one room had twelve men cooking and sleeping and sharing a cesspit in the corner that hadn't been emptied for years. You wonder how landlords get away with it.

Dr Ashburton Thompson: So far, most victims appear to be working men, which is hardly surprising given the bulk of them work on wharves where the outbreak occurred. There are thirty-six ramshackle finger wharves in varying degrees of decay, which is helping compound the problem of filth and rats. It is absolutely imperative that we deal with those persons who've had contact with plague victims so as to prevent any further spreading.

Bill Burke: Poor Mr Ah Han. Forty police went down to Chinatown round Wexford and Campbell Streets and started barricadin' people in 'cos they won't have needles. They don't understand and they're frightened. Han had his at North Head. The doctors insisted.

Jimmy Higgins: Pa's been out of work some time, but he wants to get paid on a clean-up gang. Ma's hoping he will too 'cos no one gives her washing to do now.

As for fleas, Keating's Insect Powder's meant to kill 'em but you'd need an awful lot to do a whole house, so carbolic and boiling water work out cheaper. Then there's anklets to protect you but they're only for round your ankles, so fleas'll jump straight over and up your trouser leg. I only got short pants because Ma can't afford long 'uns, so I'll spot the little buggers jumping.

Mildred Burke: We're seeing new cases all the time. Fifty yards from Palnes, a chap named Durrell, but two days later the papers said that was wrong, he lives two hundred yards away. Still too close for me.

Jimmy Higgins: I'd never been on a 'lectric tram before. Couldn't afford it but I borrowed the fare first time from Ma and since then, paid meself. You see all the carts and drays and hansoms along George Street, only the driver looked worried when I dumped me sack. Maybe he guessed it were full of rats or saw one wriggle, but he don't say nothin' on account of he don't want to scare the passengers, only he makes me swear they're dead. For a minute but, I thought I saw him scratch.

The Bathurst 'cinerator man took me bag and paid me a florin, but he don't give me back the sack. Seems some kids been takin' rats uptown, live still. So he burns the sack in case of fleas and next time says I got to put the rats in boiling water first to kill the fleas. But all animals got fleas, dogs, cats, rats. Dogs 'specially. Now I got to find a bucket with no holes for boiling.

The 'cinerator man says they're doing such good business they'll be putting 'cinerators round other spots soon, only Bathurst's my nearest.

Mrs Phillipa Dudley, wife of Captain Thomas Dudley: Our family owns a chandler business in Sussex Street near Huddart Parker Wharf and for some time now there's been a problem with the sewer and recently my husband found five dead rats in a closet he was cleaning out. We think that's probably where he caught it.

Our house is in Drummoyne and fortunately he was at home when he fell ill a few days later. He had a lump under his arm about the size of a fist that was warm and firm to the touch and he was in dreadful pain. I called the doctor immediately but there was nothing he could do and within hours Tom was dead.

Jimmy Higgins: Someone's died of it. That tall bloke with the tanned face and black beard. Moody bugger. Never talks much but has this shop selling ropes and sails and stuff. You see him down the docks sometimes and all the kids round here call him Cannibal Tom on account of he once ate someone. Fair dinkum, bones and all. He didn't die on the docks, but. He waited till he got home then carked it.

Dr Ashburton Thompson: Dr Frank Tidswell has performed an autopsy on Dudley and confirmed his death was caused by bubonic plague.

Having inspected the body and house for myself, I arranged for a total of seventeen people Dudley had had contact with, namely his family and workmates, to be sent to quarantine and for the house and shop to be placed under police guard. The body was wrapped in sailcloth soaked in five per cent sulphuric acid and buried at North Head. Dudley had reported the appalling state of the sewers in his suburb but I'm afraid that's repeated in many parts of Sydney. Only one in twenty houses is properly connected to the sewer.

Mrs Phillipa Dudley: Our two older children stayed in England after the trial, but the three younger ones are still with us and for them it's been a terrible ordeal. Having lost their father once when he was sent to prison in England, now they've lost him forever.

Jimmy Higgins: Pa's on a clean-up gang now, workin' in Grafton Street yard pulling down dunnies. They got to break up boxes and all kinds of wood for burning and remove any ironwork and chains. After that, fire engines come along and start hosin' things down, then steam dredges scoop up sludge between the wharves. Pa and his mates have to get down on hands and knees and pull out any grass growing between the wharf planks. It's filthy work and soon as he gets home, he washes all over and Ma don't let 'im come near her or us and she don't like havin' to wash his filthy clothes.

Mrs Phillipa Dudley: Tom was never the same after the trial and I curse the day he met Henry Want the politician, because that's when his troubles began. Want asked Tom to bring the *Mignonette* to Sydney when Tom knew the yacht wasn't seaworthy and said so, but he offered Tom enough to buy a cottage in Hampshire for us and Tom weakened. But what would anyone do in such circumstances? The Cornish fishermen knew and supported Tom, even clubbing together to help pay for his defence and I put all my savings towards it too.

They'd been floating for fifteen days with no food or water having to eat plankton, all the while hoping a passing ship would rescue them. Eventually, they were desperate, but by then the cabin boy was almost dead anyway.

Jimmy Higgins: My rat business is goin' real well, even though the smell's bad and passengers stare, like they think it's me that stinks.

Mrs Phillipa Dudley: His Honour, Lord Coleridge, who they called the hanging judge, was adamant it was murder and carried the death penalty, but after an appeal Tom and the first mate, Edwin Stephens, served only six months hard labour. The second mate admitted to cannibalism, but not murder, and Tom backed him on this, so he wasn't charged. In the end, Her Majesty intervened through the Home Secretary and Tom and Stephens were released.

Dr Ashburton Thompson: In the same week as Dudley died, two more cases were reported. Thankfully, the cleaning process with particular emphasis on killing rats has begun and will continue for as long as necessary. All along Kent Street, rubbish is being brought onto the roadway and taken out to sea by punt. The stench is overpowering and in some streets bonfires are lit to burn rubbish and help purify the air, but it's clear Sydney's on the brink of a large-scale outbreak. We are only two weeks into March and already we've had twenty cases.

Mrs Thomas Dudley: Tom and Stephens were treated as pariahs in prison and when they came out Tom was a changed man. We didn't want to stay in England, so Henry Want paid for us to emigrate, but Tom struggled under a black cloud he couldn't lift. I'd hoped Sydney would mean a new start, but by then, Tom had little appetite for life.

At North Head, the children and I had to watch as his coffin was placed on a two-wheeled cart and taken up a winding road to the burial ground. We weren't allowed to follow and that was as close as we came to a funeral.

My only consolation was that he died at home because from then on, he was merely a number – 48. T.R. Dudley age 49 admitted 24.2.1900. Died 24.2.1900. Diagnosed Dr Pickburn – to show that he ever existed.

Mildred Burke: We're now into March and people are starting to leave. Crowds line up at Redfern Station to catch trains for the Blue Mountains, and some going as far as Melbourne.

Of course, it's easy for those that has a house in the mountains. Harder to find somewhere to stay if you don't.

Our neighbours, McCanns at 86 Windmill have lost their daughter, Elleanor Matilda. Lovely girl, everyone called her Nellie. She went to Lower Fort Street Public, but on 16th she come home complaining of terrible headache and vomiting, and her mother, Alice, called Dr Hodgson. He came around noon and left a prescription, but an hour later Nellie was dead.

So sad seein' her taken off to the City Morgue. I didn't know what to say to her parents. The post-mortem said it was plague, so they had to pack up the others, Bertie, Wilfred, Ethel and Ruby, and go to North Head, where Nellie was buried.

George Taylor, Government Pathologist: I initially diagnosed the McCann girl as having died of acute septicaemia, so I was greatly surprised to discover from subsequent tests that she'd died of plague. A few days later, I went to the Board of Health office but was barred entry and decided they must think I was still infectious from the girl's death, but they assured me it was for my own safety, because a large crowd had stormed the offices in a panic wanting inoculations.

Mildred Burke: There's been two more deaths and a queue in Macquarie Street for needles right out over the pavement. The crush inside were so bad a glass noticeboard was smashed and part of a wooden staircase gave way. The doctors gave hundreds of needles but it's not enough.

It's been nearly two weeks, so I went over the road to see the Mc-Canns now they're back. Alice is really down, poor love, on account of they weren't allowed to go to Nellie's funeral and can't afford a headstone, so their little girl is in an unmarked grave. She says the younger children are very upset, it being so sudden and Nellie the eldest, like a little mother to them.

Bill Burke: All over Sydney there's talk of cleanin' up. Which suburbs are done and which'll be next and gangs mostly doing a good job. There's teams in Annandale and out as far as Vaucluse and they've cordoned off streets like Kent, for about a mile along the foreshore.

Barricades went up very early before anyone was out of bed, so people just found 'em there. Now there's a curfew to make sure no one goes out without proper reason and has to be back before dark. It's like being in the army and the worst thing is people aren't allowed to go to jobs. The papers are sayin' the area should have been cordoned off ages ago. The delay's because the Colonial Secretary owns a store in the area. Doesn't surprise me.

George McCredie, Consulting Engineer Department of Public Works: As of 23 March, I've been put in charge of quarantine arrangements. It'll be my job to inspect all houses in plague areas and within the quarantined zone. I'll also be supervising cleansing and demolition of houses and properties where necessary. To that end, I've engaged a man to photograph all premises destined for cleansing or demolition to avoid any litigation or prosecution by landlords at some future date.

Jimmy Higgins: There's a new notice up: PROCLAMATION PLAGUE in big letters and if you sees lots of dead rats, you got to tell the coppers. Another sign says they'll now pay 2d a head for every rat (dead or alive) taken to Bathurst Street. At tuppence a rat, I'll get rich faster and Ma's given me a bucket with only a bit of a dent but no hole to boil 'em in. When I take 'em uptown on the tram, fleas won't be sizin' up the passengers. Trouble is, Rosie always wants to help with rat hunting, as she calls it. I tell her it's not a job for girls, but she says she can do anyfink boys can do, so I'm stuck. She picks 'em up by the tail and says, 'ere's one, Jimmy! every couple of minutes and I go and take it from her and tell her to wipe her hands on 'er pinny 'cos they're fithly dirty and she's to let me grab them, then she goes and does it again. Drives me mad, only she gets bored just watching and she knows I get money for 'em and that means more aniseed cats for her.

J.F. Vincent, Superintendent of Quarantine, North Head: It's my job to issue stores at the station. I help supervise the manning of launches and fumigation of mail and oversee labouring and other duties. These vary considerably. Recently, a boy of the surname Macie was due for release, but he was homeless, so I kept him at the station until arrangements could be made for his long-term care. He gave no trouble and frankly we've had adults who've given far more, refusing to give their names or arriving at the station, drunk. We have no proper gaol, but a shed near the wharf is big enough to retain difficult contacts until they come to their senses or sober up.

Bill Burke: There's another case in Sussex Street and a chap named Walker in Annandale. But closer to home, Clarence Street's being cleaned. The boarding houses along it were overflowing with sailors and wharfies, sometimes as many as seventy crammed into six rooms. So of course, plague's going to spread. Besides, there's still rats everywhere, even in street sweepings out as far as Wentworthville.

Mildred Burke: More houses are up for sale all over Sydney, in Newtown, Stanmore, Enmore even Dulwich Hill, then on the east side, posh suburbs like Darlinghurst and Darling Point and a house at 75 Cascade Street, Paddington, with a loft and stables too.

Bill Burke: And it's not just houses for sale. Plenty of businesses and lots of people ruined. Some folks refuse to go near anyone that's had plague or been in contact, so businesses suffer. There's adverts for butter runs, restaurants, even mercery shops.

Mildred Burke: More people are fallin' sick all the time. We're still in March and a family named Dovey over Moore Park way has come down with it. And down Goulburn Street some houses have kitchens and water closets joined together. In nearby Robertsons Lane, there's anything from six to ten boarders crammed in one small room and charged sixpence a night and if that's not bad enough, some have extra rooms tacked on as well.

After the stampede in Macquarie Street, the Board of Health's opened a new needle centre in Prince Alfred Park in the Exhibition Building, so hopefully there won't be another panic. Bill and I had our needles at North Head, but another 1,200 people yesterday had their sleeves rolled up, waiting. Over three thousand so far.

Dr Asburton Thompson: I must make it clear I've no reason in supposing the Dovey children were infected at the Quarantine Station. On the contrary, I've every reason to think they were infected at home before they arrived. As a precaution, however, I've inspected the Quarantine Station and appointed two more nurses from the Coast Hospital to cope with the number of cases.

The Doveys live at Baptist Gardens, Redfern, within a hundred yards of Moore Park tip. Neighbours have said the children are in the habit of going to the tip despite Mrs Dovey insisting this is not the case. I've been told there are plenty of rats in the street and in their house as well, which had a plague of fleas. The children are covered with the remains of flea bites not a quarter of an inch apart.

Bill Burke: That chap from Sussex Street died on Monday and the Annandale man, Walker, yesterday. Henry Casson, who lives not far from the Doveys in Redfern, has come down with it too.

All round here the government's sent men to inspect houses, yards and water closets. It's not nice having to put up with strangers swarming over your house, like you haven't bothered to keep it clean, but it's their job.

Dr Ashburton Thompson: Moore Park tip has been a major problem. Rotten produce from the wharves has been dumped there for years and local children scavenge for fruit, mainly bananas. The tipping of refuse must cease immediately and all deposits of rubbish, old and new, should be carefully sprinkled by water carts with a mixture of water and sulphuric acid. If such steps are taken, there'll be nothing for the rats to eat, which of course means they'll spread out looking for food, so everyone must kill any rats they catch. As of today, I am pleased to report Moore Park tip has finally been closed.

I'm also sorry to report the youngest member of the Dovey family did not die at the station. The body was delivered from Sydney Hospital, where he'd been taken, and the whole family is now in quarantine.

Frederick Dovey aged two, died 10 March 1900 at Sydney Hospital and is buried at the Quarantine Station, North Head.

Mildred Burke: We've heard from George. He came round Sunday to tell us about his new job. He's working for an undertaker making coffins all day, there's such a demand. He not only makes them, he goes with his boss on the funeral cart down to Cowper Wharf, where the coffins get taken to North Head. He's doin' something useful but hates the way people step back from the kerb when they see the cart go past with UNDERTAKER on the side. Some even curse, or cross theirselves.

Dr Ashburton Thompson: Captain Downes, Maritime Superintendent of A.U.S.N. Company, says the water in Darling Harbour is filthy. When the wind is westerly, the drift of decaying animal and vegetable matter ends up around the piles of wharves along Sussex Street, which is appalling to health. Last week, he saw ten dead fish, part of a side of beef, several dead fowls, one or two dead dogs besides other bodies, including dead rats, all packed into a space of about twelve foot square. It was so disgusting he gave orders for the whole lot to be towed out to sea. He says many of the company's employees suffered from typhoid last year, so something must be done about it.

It's an uphill battle, but we're doing whatever we can to improve the situation. We have three thousand men cleaning up and working systematically through each street and laneway in The Rocks, covering every house and business. Many are being pulled down, being beyond repair, and new drains and water closets installed. It's my hope with such stringent procedures we'll eventually gain the upper hand.

Annie French: We got a proper bathroom now out back, with bath and cold-water tap, chip heater and all. The pipe goes through the fire box and, after a bit, hot water comes out. Only I got more work puttin' in wood and cleanin' out ash, but it's worth it. It smokes a bit and stung our eyes till I got Jimmy to find a pair of old automobile goggles to wear.

Jimmy Higgins: There's this chap takes photos of houses and sometimes he lets us kids stand there while he does. He sets up a camera on three legs and gets everything ready then says to keep still and not move or we'll have blurry faces, but it's hard for littlies to keep still that long. Rosie kept squirming and wriggling,, sayin' she had to spend a penny.

He says havin' us in the photo helps show how tall houses are but once word gets out, people come running to get their photo took. Once, he had us all lined up to Whalers Arms pub.

Mrs Higgins: Jimmy says he and Rosie had their photo took by a stranger and I said, What stranger? and he said, Some man as lives in Balmain. It's his job to photo all the houses round. Why's he got to take pictures of kiddies? He might be peculiar, but Jimmy says he's from Public Works, so I s'pose that makes him all right.

Mildred Burke: We bumped into a neighbour yesterday and the dear old thing was beside herself. She said the cleaning gang had been drinking before they turned up and they limewashed her piano she's had since she were a girl, but Bill said rats make nests anywhere, even in pianos. I told him that didn't help.

Today, I had my photo taken, first time since Bill and me were married. I'd seen this photographer chap round, but he caught me off guard when he asked would I like to stand still with another neighbour at the top of Ferry Lane, chatting like. Then this copper come up looking ever so dashin' in his cape and cap and he was asked to be in it too. Then a little girl come up with her skipping rope and was about to skip down Windmill Street when he said, Stop! That's perfect. Keep still! so we did. He must get tired of takin' photos of houses all day long but I wish he'd have let me go home and change me pinny. I'd only stepped out for a minute and must have looked a proper sight all tossed and windblown like an old sailing ship.

Bill Burke: Every day, ratcatchers are out and about with their cages and baits and Foxies and little Jack Russells. They carry billycans with lids for boiling water and the piles of rats get so big you'd hardly imagine there'd be that many for only a few hours' work. One man said he's found dozens of new burrows since last night in one small area alone and that means at least forty or fifty down each. If you count three or four rats for every human, soon there'll be a hundred to one because females have about ten litters a year and mostly ten to a litter. Rats are filthy. The catchers say they've got dark waxy oil on their fur that leaves black stains when they run along walls and since they don't have bladders, like, they dribble. That's what leaves the awful smell.

The catchers are flat out trying everything; dogs, traps, baits. They even put burning sulphur down sewers to get rid of them. The other day they had their picture taken with their traps and cages and dogs. Normally they're heading down a drain so fast you can't stop 'em. But this time, the dogs knew their photo was being took and stood still.

Mildred Burke: Quarantine is really hard on some families when the breadwinner can't get out to work. None of the coal-lumpers or wharfies can work with the wharves closed and some families have sick rellies to care for as well.

Poor Mr Ah Han hasn't been round for ages. So many people are blaming the Chinese for the plague, so maybe he's better off staying in Chinatown for a while.

Bill Burke: A group of us went up to Parliament House in Macquarie Street yesterday to see Mr Hughes, our local member. We waited outside for ages demanding to see him and in the end a guard went and got him. He'd been arguing with Premier Lyne, who doesn't think there's a problem! Or he says plague's our problem not his.

The Hon. William Morris Hughes, Member NSW Legislative Assembly: I wish to state publicly how appalled I am at the condition of housing in central and harbourside Sydney. I will do my utmost to reform the Sydney City Council and try to improve the situation for people living in the vicinity. The premier's solution is to put up barricades in certain areas and send in clean-up gangs, but this is not fair on men with jobs on the outside, unable to work. I am insisting that men inside cordoned off areas be allowed to form their own clean-up gangs. That way, at least they'll be paid.

Bill Burke: Today, Mr Hughes himself come and all these people were lined up our side of the barricades with him on the other. He's only short, so with people yelling and heckling, he had to shout to be heard. He's been telling the premier to pay six shillings a day to men who can't get out to work, but so far the premier's said No, only the premier's agreed to see for hisself. Not close enough to get bitten, mind, but from a boat.

Jimmy Higgins: Something's been killing fish in the Harbour. There's thousands floating dead on the surface. Bream, leatherjackets, whiting, all sorts, even flathead. Only it can't be plague that's killin' them 'cos fish don't get fleas. Fish plague, maybe?

Bill Burke: There was a riot this morning in Bates Lane. People waving sticks and cudgels when Premier Lyne tried to send in his clean-up gangs from outside. They began pouring lime over a cottage and those living there were hopping mad. Not surprised. So a scuffle broke out and soon all the neighbours joined in and several got their heads smashed and some trampled almost to death in the crush.

But at least Mr Lyne's seen for hisself. His boat went past the bottom of Erskine Street and he saw hundreds and hundreds of rats running up and down the wharf piles. Since then Mr Hughes has made him promise to pay local men eight shillings a day on clean-up, so that's good even though it must be hard on some poor buggers having to stand by and see their houses pulled down.

Men not on gangs get a special dole to stay this side till it's over, but some buggers outside have jumped over, hoping to get the dole this side.

Jimmy Higgins: Mr Burke says it's the stuff they're washing the houses with, lysol, carbolic and sulphuric acid, running down the drains into the Harbour that's killing fish. I had to stop Rosie taking a couple home for tea thinkin' Ma'd be pleased, but they looked funny to me.

John Degotardi, photographer, Department of Public Works: I had no idea how huge a job it would be and how disheartening. I've taken streetscapes down to the harbour showing ships, but when I photograph houses, I feel moved knowing so many are marked for demolition. The least I can do is include some of those who live there, since many will never have had their photo taken.

But I try and avoid stiff portraits. I prefer to capture people in their everyday lives where they appear natural. The children are delightful, often with their billycarts or wagons, and smaller boys who can't wait to run off and play barely keep still long enough for the plate to take.

The little girls are more willing to pose with their dollies, and older girls are often carrying a younger sister or brother, but manage to hold hands with younger ones or sometimes try to twirl their skirts for the camera.

Mildred Burke: Anthony Hordern has a sale of mourning clothes, like they're expecting lots of funerals, but I got one black dress that does weddings and funerals alike and a coat. Besides, I don't want to jinx the neighbours.

Another Dovey child's come down with plague, a seven-year-old this time, so that's four in that family. And other names keep popping up. John Butler, 24, and Alexander Bell, who's 18. Total strangers but once their names are printed, they seem real somehow.

Bill Burke: It's been bad enough seeing notices about rats. Now there's one up saying stray dogs seen wandering about will be put down, but what if it's someone's pet, or a catcher's little Jack Russell that gets out his yard and is caught?

The noise of clean-up is driving us mad. All day long, sledgehammers banging and crashing against walls. Carts and drays full of rubbish rumbling down to the wharves and the constant hiss and whine of steam engines parked along Kent Street spraying walls and yards and all the while their funnels belchin' out grimy black smoke

Parts of Sydney have become a ghost town, with theatres and hotels closed, shops and markets and everywhere this awful smell of carbolic and lime being painted on fences and walls. We'll be glad when it's all over.

John Degotardi: I'm starting to feel I know these people and they regard me almost as a friend because I spend time with them, seeing their living conditions. In my own small way, I think of myself as an artist of sorts and they my figures in the landscape. Sometimes I include myself in frame, setting up the camera and racing round to the front. You can tell it's me in the boater or holding my pipe.

Photography is all about composition, so I look at a scene trying to imagine how it will look through the lens, allowing for the sweep up a hill, the way a street is framed by houses either side. For one photograph, I showed the upper and lower levels of a road like an arrowhead, positioning my tripod where the streets converged. As for showing endless rows of depressing backyards, I try to show them in patterns, piled one on top of another, but it still doesn't diminish the squalor.

Dr Ashburton Thompson: We've recently passed a high mortality peak during which accommodation at North Head was stretched to the limit. I've therefore approached the government suggesting contacts be allowed to stay in their own homes as long as they're quarantined and under surveillance and have been inoculated as well. This would help ease the pressure on the Quarantine Station. The premier, however, has refused, his argument being that unless a strict system is enforced on rich and poor alike, he will be accused of favouritism. The most he will agree to is the number of days contacts are held at North Head be reduced from ten to five. Hopefully, this will relieve a little of the congestion, since the hospital is full to capacity and many contacts have had to be housed in tents to allow for convalescing patients to be moved into more durable buildings normally used for contacts.

As an extra measure, the premier has also arranged for two pavilions to be erected on site. They'll contain bedrooms, another dining room and water closets, and are apparently to be named Lyne's Buildings, in his honour.

John Degotardi, photographer: On days I photograph backyards, I go home feeling wretched that such poverty can exist. Many dwellings have back-to-back WCs and at No. 2 Walton Place I found a small girl standing barefoot in a filthy yard near the door of an appalling privy. I felt like scooping her up and taking her home, although how my wife and children would react, I can only imagine. At 129 Gloucester Street, another little girl stood holding her baby sister and smiling as she was photographed, oblivious of the dreadful conditions around her. She had no idea the privies were scheduled for demolition next day.

Another little mite at 135 George Street looked suspiciously at me, refusing to move out of frame as if she were guarding her home, when all I wanted was to photograph her backyard.

The whole pattern of backyards seems one of make-do and add-on, with lean-tos often patched with sheets of tin or planks of odd wood to ward off the elements. In places where there are no backyards such as Clyde Street, which is barely twelve feet wide, washing is strung out on pulley ropes across the street.

Bill Burke: Some smart alec's written in the *Arrow* that humiliation and prayer aren't much use without cremation and disinfectant. I don't go to church meself but if it gives people comfort at a time like this, then why not?

But you want to avoid Bible-bashers thumping pulpits. One's been saying plague is a divine visitation against the shameless violation of the Sabbath, gambling and intemperance. Next, he'll be saying God created rats and fleas as part of His divine plan.

Mildred Burke: We're into April now and plague's still with us. Any case has to be reported straight away and infected bedding and clothing destroyed. Schools and places people meet are being cleaned and purified at the owners' expense. But who owns churches, I wonder? They're called Houses of God, but it'll be Catlicks, Protty Dogs, Baptists and Wesleyans as pays for cleaning.

Some churches asked to hold a Day of Humiliation on 12 April but the Colonial Secretary said the date's been booked already for the opening of the Royal Easter Show.

Bill Burke: The government should never have let things get this bad. You need light and air round a house so those inside can breathe and have space to hang out washing or grow a few chokos. But the way some owners tack rooms on the back of houses is downright wrong. Just shows how greedy some are, the way some landlords fill backyards in with more houses. So No. 195 1/2 Cumberland Street is inside 195's backyard and next door, 197 1/2 is hard up against No. 197. That's land sweating and illegal but it still goes on.

We were lucky our house weren't pulled down but we had to doss down on the floor of Ragged School in Harrington Street while the smell of carbolic and lime was bad. The Salvos and City Mission looked after us and gave us clean blankets and pillows and plenty of tea and sandwiches. They couldn't have persuaded Mildred unless she got her cups of tea. She's a six-cup-a-day girl and even then she was missing her favourite teapot.

Jimmy Higgins: Ma's bought me and Rosie some of them flea anklets. Not Pa, she says he stinks so bad of carbolic the fleas won't go near him. She's told Rosie they're like socks only I ain't never worn socks in boots, so they feel kind of funny and I still reckon the fleas'll jump over 'em.

Mildred Burke: The plague has all sorts of people helping out. A lady doctor from Tasmania, Sadie Morie, knows all about plague after working in India. Now she's working here for the government.

But even with all the doctors and nurses working hard, people are still dying. Andrew Mills, twenty-four, from Leichhardt yesterday, and today would have been his wedding. He went to quarantine on 25 March and his fiancée was a contact. She pleaded to be able to nurse him but wasn't allowed. It's quarantine rules, but now he's dead she won't be having a wedding day.

Two more died today.

Bill Burke: I can't believe there's still ads for cures. Plague! The Black Death! The Scourge of the East! Take Dr Morse's Indian Root Pills and avoid it! As if they'd help. How do they get away with it? The government should ban them 'cos they only build up people's hopes and make them feel safe.

Mildred Burke: More cases, one on the North Shore, one in the city, two in Waverley, so it's still spreading and with all these names being printed, will their neighbours avoid them when they come back?

The open sewer from George Street to Blackwattle Bay's been covered over but so many rats were found in Wexford Street they've sent in a clean-up gang specially. Chinese men offered to work on it, but weren't allowed, which isn't fair when they're barricaded in with no earnings.

Jimmy Higgins: The Bathurst 'cinerator is almost worn out, so they'll have to get a new one. They know me so well now, they let me throw the rats in meself.

Mildred Burke: Someone in Woolloomooloo has it, and a little girl named Emily Shaw was taken to the Children's Hospital feeling sick and her parents were told she had it, so they all went to quarantine.

And Mary Boshell from the Caledonian Hotel in King Street lost her only son yesterday. Three and a half, in quarantine only two days before she caught it, but he died the night before she was admitted, so she never saw him again.

Bill Burke: I never thought when Arthur Paine fell sick in January, we'd still be seeing cases at Easter but it's now Good Friday, only none of the fish'll be coming from Sydney Harbour, but from Brisbane Waters, where there's no disinfectant. Thank goodness.

Mildred Burke: It's come on awfully cold all of a sudden. Freezing. I had to dig out my warm coat. The coldest Easter for forty-one years they're saying, with rain squalls and gales. The only good thing is, not as many are falling sick, the lowest number of cases since it started, because it seems rats don't like cold weather so they've cleared off.

Some stinkers have gone down to Chinatown and attacked people in the streets throwing stones. One man's killed himself because his business was ruined with no money coming in. But they've just as much right to be here as anyone.

Bill Burke: The big shops are having sales, with ads for bicycles saying you don't have to catch a tram and insurance companies are offering policies against plague. They might help your family if you die but won't stop you gettin' it.

Mildred Burke: Two more cases in Summer Hill and Paddington but at least the clean-up gangs have finished round here and the smell's gone from the house, so we're back in. I was gettin' sick of tea and sandwiches and missed me Brown Betty teapot. Tea's not the same from one of them big metal teapots.

Barricades are down in Kent and Druitt Streets though some still up in Sussex and Liverpool.

Sixty-two poor souls still sick in quarantine.

Dr Ashburton Thompson: I'd no wish to cause panic but that's exactly what happened when authorities tried to remove forty patrons from the Grosvenor Hotel in Ultimo recently. There was a confrontation, with some patrons refusing to go to quarantine when asked. They had to be forcibly removed from the premises and one man managed to escape and got as far as Goulburn before he was found and brought back to Sydney then sent to North Head.

Bill Burke: More and more businesses are up for sale. You can buy a grocer's, or butcher's, or confectioner's and further out round Parramatta, even a five-acre farm with chooks. I quite like the idea and five acres is probably all I could manage. But we don't see much of George now and it'd be less out there. Besides, Mildred would never agree. I can't see her happy talking to chooks all day long

But all this time, chemist shops are doing very well selling cures, and plumbers are run off their feet connecting houses to the sewer.

Mr Richard Whitehead, Borambil Station, Condobolin: Maggie and I were holidaying in Sydney at the Grosvenor when she suddenly became ill. We had no idea plague had swept through the hotel till there was a hullabaloo one night when police descended and started carting people off to quarantine. That was 29 April and Maggie was among those diagnosed, so we were both sent to North Head. I was given the vaccine, but she was taken straight to hospital, where I wasn't allowed to see her. I didn't even have time to say good-bye and four days later she was dead. It was seven thirty in the morning. I'll never forget because I'd gone for a walk and stopped to look at the view across the harbour. There are rough paths through the banksia and melaleuca scrub. I was angry at not being allowed to see her and having to rely on doctors to keep me informed. But that morning, I saw a nurse walking towards me and knew immediately why she was there.

I can't blame the doctors, they did all they could, but I would have preferred to take her home to Condobolin to bury her. There's a peaceful spot under a shady white gum she loved, but sadly it wasn't to be. They were adamant as to how she had to be buried with stringent disinfecting measures, in a deeper than usual grave.

I arranged for a Presbyterian minister, Rev. Allan McDougall, to conduct the service and was told a couple of nurses attended. McDougall didn't know Maggie, but we talked beforehand, and the nurses said he did a good job, considering. I found it hard not being allowed to attend, but they tell me are clumps of flowering tea trees and grevillea all around and she would have liked that.

Before I returned home, I ordered a headstone:

In Fond Remembrance of MAGGIE the beloved wife of RICHARD WHITEHEAD Borambil Station, Condobolin, who died in quarantine May 3rd, 1900 of Bubonic Plague Aged 40 Years. Contacted in Sydney.

Mr J.F. Vincent, Superintendent: Some of those buried at the station have had hard lives, with no family to mourn them. Edward Edney was 48, employed as a servant at 470 Riley Street, Surry Hills, and sixteen-year-old Peter Rafferty from 359 Harris Street, Pyrmont, was quarantined on 2 May, died at five thirty p.m., 3 May, and was buried at three a.m. the following day, Father Ignatius officiating. We try to conduct burials late at night or in the early hours so as not to upset contacts. Sometimes, I have to conduct a burial service myself if I can't find a clergyman of the deceased's faith in time.

Mr Richard Whitehead, Borambil Station: I was angry when I ordered that last line, because I still feel she'd be alive if we'd stayed at home. It wasn't my idea to come down, especially since we're in the middle of one of the worst droughts we've had for years and I can't afford to lose any more stock. But I could see it was distressing her, looking out day after day over scorched paddocks, seeing dead sheep. She found it upsetting and kept saying she needed to get to Sydney, back to the harbour, so I agreed.

In the end, I couldn't have asked for a lovelier setting in which to bury my darling wife. It is far enough away from the noise and bustle of the city but looks out across that vast expanse of water. I like to imagine the feeling of peace with hardly a sound except maybe the call of a lonely currawong.

Bill Burke: It's much cooler now, which you'd expect given it's autumn, but even so, there are five more cases, from all over Sydney and one from Chinatown. The council's talking of building a morgue for those dying in the city that they plan to put it at Dawes or Millers Point. Over my dead body. Who wants a morgue on their doorstep? Anyway, I thought those as died of plague have to be taken to North Head.

Over in Botany, a Chinese man caught plague so the council demanded to see all the houses there. Well, not all the houses, only those lived in by Chinese. They had to admit the houses were perfectly clean inside, just terrible outside, and no human beings should have to live in houses with no proper drains.

Ah Han has sent a note saying if he and his family end up with nowhere to live, he'll be looking to put up a couple of packing cases in someone's backyard and moving in. I think he was joking, and he didn't say our backyard, but it'd be a bit of a squeeze. Still, I guess we'd manage somehow. He's also worried about his horse, how's he going to feed him if he can't find work, and we definitely don't have room for a horse. Hopefully, things are getting back to normal, so he'll soon be on the road again.

Jimmy Higgins: There's a new notice up outside the grocer's that sells Rosie's aniseed cats. Two for a farthing or six for a penny, she keeps remindin' me. The government's now payin' 6d a rat! It's not nice to think of people dying, but the rats have got to be killed and I hope it goes on just a little longer so I can sell more. Ma thinks it's shockin' that much for a bleedin' rat, but I told her it's 'cos they're harder to find and now to get 'em up to Bathurst you got to take them in billy-cans with lids and disinfectant – six per cent corrosive sublimate. I asked Mr Burke and he said that's glycerine and muriatic acid added to water up to a gallon. Then you got to take 'em out with tongs once they're in there. That means I got to buy a couple of cans with lids and stuff for soaking and tongs. It'll have to come out of me savings but can't be helped.

Bill Burke: Only one case yesterday and seven this week, the lowest for some time and ten patients have been let go from North Head. But seven hundred rats were still killed this week and 167 in other suburbs. They think probably more 'n 68,000 have been killed since the beginning of March. I can't imagine a pile that big but I'm glad young Jimmy's doing his bit. I see him heading for the tram with his load, but he tells me he's being sensible and boiling 'em first.

Mildred Burke: It's June now, so the start of winter, which means we've been battling plague for six months. Another six cases were reported on Saturday but none yesterday, and two more deaths in hospital, James Wilson, a one-year-old baby, and Richard Jones, a lad of seventeen.

Two others, besides, are critical.

Bill Burke: A new case yesterday and another today, just when I was starting to think it was over. The harbour's still closed, and no one's allowed to fish or bathe because of carbolic and dead fish. The smell of rotting on top of everything else is dreadful.

I ran into Jimmy's pa today. His gang's been working along George Street cleanin' out shops. He says there's butchers' premises with open cesspits out the yard and strings of sausages hanging over chopping blocks, not to mention privies with no doors and several like that he says. Sutton Forest Butchery at 761 George and another at 841 both bad as each other, with ox kidneys, hearts and tripe left lying on benches covered in flies straight from the dunny and big tubs of smallgoods with only a layer of fat for cover. And the floor's covered in sawdust brown with old blood. Puts me off sausages.

Mildred Burke: A little girl, Lilian Stephens, has come down with it and a man died over in quarantine. In Manly, clean-up gangs pulled down a house and found thirty dead rats rotting under the floorboards. The smell was so bad the men kept rushing out for a gulp of fresh air before going back in.

Bill Burke: Halfway through June we had another four cases and by the end of the month another three. I've lost count how many have caught it and it's not done yet. I can't help but think of the poor people buried at North Head. It's not like an ordinary cemetery where you can go and take flowers.

Mildred Burke: No new cases for eight days now and no one dead from quarantine, so fingers crossed.

Meanwhile, Mutual Stores in Pitt Street are having a Mid-Winter

'Plague' Sale of Ladies' Cloaks and Furs. It don't sound like things women round here would wear.

Jimmy Higgins: Pa's finished on clean-up and now he's a scavenger getting rubbish out the harbour. So far, he says, they've pulled 1,006 dead rats, 504 dogs, 300 chooks, 279 cats not counting other animals like pigs and sheep. Cats and dogs maybe, if you don't want another litter, but dead sheep?

When there's no more rubbish to collect, Pa says he's thinking of being a rag and bone man. He'll soon have enough for a horse and cart, they're goin' real cheap and he says I can go into business with him. I can't wait.

Bill Burke: No one's come down with plague for three weeks but there's a really sick man at North Head still and a chap named William Montague turned up to Sydney Hospital feeling crook and they were suspicious and sent him to quarantine, where there's three others sick with it.

Jimmy Higgins: There's still rats about, but not as many. Catchers used to get 900 a day, now it's more like 350. Catchers have killed around 71,000 since January they say. But it bein' winter, the rats have mostly cleared off, so the Foxies are getting a holiday.

Mr J.F. Vincent, Superintendent: We've had no new cases at the station now for a whole month, the last person to die was Robert West from 64 Greek Street, Glebe. He was fifty-eight and died on 18 August, the same day two Catholic priests, a Presbyterian and an Anglican minister were told their services were no longer required and their pay would be stopped. Fortunately, I was able to detain the Anglican, Rev John Moran to stay long enough to conduct West's funeral.

There have been so many deaths and burials, and it must have been hard on the clergy with no weddings or baptisms in between. Most burials have been of men, but sometimes a woman was interred and saddest of all were the children some of whom were very young. It's not as if they died from accidents or childhood sicknesses. Plague is something parents would not have anticipated, and it must have been so much more distressing when they couldn't be present at the graveside.

Head Nurse Ford, Quarantine Station: Now that the epidemic appears to have run its course, I'd like to say how proud I am of my nurses. They've worked tirelessly and unstintingly, always putting their patients first, despite an ever-present risk to themselves. It's thanks in part to their long hours and devoted service we've been able to keep the mortality figures comparatively low. My only regret is having to remain firm and insist on no communication between contacts and patients because of the risk of spreading. This has caused great pain, I know, especially with burials, but it's a rule we've had to enforce.

George McCredie, Chief Organiser Quarantine Procedures: I kept a map of the city in my office and put a black mark for every plague victim so I could see how densely affected some areas were. It first appeared at the water's edge then travelled east up the ridge running north south parallel with Darling Harbour and finishing on York Street. From there, it went down the other side to George Street, up the eastern side as far as Elizabeth, where it stayed briefly at the intersection of Liverpool and Elizabeth Streets before moving on.

The entire cost of clean-up we estimate to have been £63,935 with between one thousand and three thousand men employed. It was completed by17 July and in that time 1,750 people were evacuated. There was no authority that gave us permission to do this, but we felt the gravity of the situation necessitated making decisions and proceeding without.

We're pleased a comparatively small number of people died, but at least 10,700 were inoculated and 3,808 buildings cleaned. Huge piles of timber were burned, and fowl houses, stables and outhouses razed to the ground. A total of 1,423 dead animals were removed from the

Harbour plus 52,030 tons of silt and sewage from the front of wharves. We dumped 28,455 tons of rubbish out to sea and burnt a further 25,430 tons and more than a million rats were killed.

Dr Ashburton Thompson: I cannot stress the importance of sufficient sanitation laws as the best protection for a city against plague. No other general scheme of defence is practicable. Dangerous conditions for the most part wouldn't occur under good municipal government. As of 31 October, I can report that Haffkine's vaccine, although not a hundred per cent effective, has helped significantly to reduce the mortality rate. Once our second batch arrived in mid-March we were able to offer vaccination to the wider public and on our heaviest day a thousand people were inoculated by two doctors in six hours. As soon as supplies ran out, more were ordered from overseas.

George McCredie: Initially, we thought only working-class men were affected with the greatest number of deaths of men between fifteen and forty-five, a number of whom had worked in wharf areas. Infected shipboard rats mingled with wharfside rats and by late February, city rats were also infected. From wharf warehouses, drays and carts took sacks of grain, hay and produce to factories in the suburbs, so the disease spread, and then not only working-class men were affected.

Arthur Casson was a librarian from the Public Library, Arthur Ross a clerk with the Bank of New Zealand, Horace Jones a clerk in William Street, while Norman Brown was an actor at Her Majesty's Theatre. The range of occupations was wider than at first thought, just as suburbs affected extended across Sydney.

Suburbs that registered cases included Darling Harbour, Pyrmont, Balmain, then to the east, Redfern, Surry Hills, Woolloomooloo and Paddington. Beyond the city were Alexandria, Waterloo, Ultimo, Botany, Camperdown, Newtown, Glebe, Marrickville and Canterbury. There were also cases across the Harbour at Kirribilli, North Sydney, on to North Rocks, with a total of five cases in Manly.

Dr Ashburton Thompson: We were indebted to a French doctor, Dr Alexandre Yersin, from the Institut Pasteur and to a Japanese scientist Dr Kitasato Shibasaburo, who were in Hong Kong during the epidemic in 1894. Both identified the plague bacillus, *Yersinia pestis*. Ten thousand people died in Hong Kong, from where it spread to Bombay, where another French doctor, Paul Simond, was working and suggested a possible connection between rats and fleas and the latter as the likely vector. I was of course aware of their work, so was on my guard should an outbreak occur in Sydney which is why we were able to act so quickly.

However, only some species of fleas transmit the disease to humans. *Xenopsylla cheopis* prefers warmer climates like Sydney and Queensland, so Melbourne, Tasmania and New Zealand reported relatively few cases. The peak breeding season for these fleas is February to March, which is significant when you consider the increases in cases over that period. The two highest peaks of morbidity were from 23 March to 12 April, and from 20 April to 17 May, the worst period being week twelve, from 6 April to 12 April.

I sympathise with families disrupted and devastated, but as with most epidemics, plague brought out the best and worst in people and by far the worst behaviour was metered out to Chinese. A Citizens Vigilante Committee did good work encouraging the public to take an interest in cleaning up and getting rid of rats, but some members went too far, taking a draconian approach in fumigating Chinese houses, when people are forced to live in crowded dirty areas. Yet the houses themselves were often exemplary in their internal cleanliness.

I am also ashamed to say the Board of Health insisted on Chinese patients in quarantine being housed separately in tents apart from Caucasian patients. This was completely unacceptable, but I was powerless to stop it. There was no particular reason for this, other than the old-established idea that Chinese, together with Indians, Negroes and other races who subsist mostly on a vegetable diet, have less resistance to disease than other nations.

Mildred Burke: Jimmy's a good lad. He's been out all hours collecting rats to earn money and today he took his ma a bunch of flowers. First she's ever had. She says he's got a good business head on his shoulders and she hopes he'll do something in life.

Dr Ashburton Thompson: It's been a difficult and harrowing time for doctors. They've had to deal with very sick people making sure they didn't become infected, and many have found themselves shunned by the public. In some cases, walking down the street carrying their black bags had people standing back or turning away. Such ignorance and rudeness I find appalling. They were only performing their duty and deserved to be treated with respect.

Officially, 103 people have died out of 303 who were infected, but the actual number of deaths could well be much higher as it's thought many cases may have gone undiagnosed or were misdiagnosed. Elleanor McCann was believed to have died of blood poisoning, but it turned out she had plague, so how many other cases were also registered incorrectly?

Bill Burke: Mr Ah Han come round today with his dray of fruit and veg so we asked him in for a cup of tea. He's glad to be back in business but his horse needs fattening, so Mildred gave it a crust of bread and jam and a carrot, and I said I'd put in a good word for Ah Han round here. If he can find enough work, he can move back.

George has asked for his old room back. We've not let it out again since our lodger left and he'll says he'll pay almost as much each week and I won't have to put up another stencil. He says he don't want another boarding house, but I think it's 'cos he plans to be nearer Annie.

We had 'em round for tea Sunday, it being Annie's birthday. Mildred made tripe and onions and very tasty, plus a cake for afters. Annie's too young to get married at seventeen. But this way they'll maybe save a bit of money and next year when she turns eighteen, who knows?

Mildred Burke: Jimmy's found me a kitten. I'd asked him to keep a lookout and somebody left a bag with a litter in the middle of the road for a cart to run over. I don't know what's worse that or drowning. Anyway, the rest of the litter was dead, but he saw the bag move and one little mite was still alive. I were that pleased when Jimmy turned up, I give him a tanner. It's a tabby like Tibbles and looks like a fighter, so I've called him Tiger and if any rats come round again, they'll have him to answer to.

Jimmy Higgins: The plague's finally over and they're not buyin' rats no more. But with my savings I plan to buy a big bag of marbles, good ones, too. You can get glass ones in different sizes, so some cat's eyes and tom bowlers and maybe some tronks, dobbers and toebreakers. I'll make sure Rosie don't play with them, but she can have what's left of my old ones.

Letter in a Strange Hand

BUDAPEST: Archaeologists think they may have found the remains of a 15th-century witch in a grave at Csenger in Hungary. The skeleton, which showed an 'extremely strange' shaped head, was found lying on its side. The burial is regarded as particularly unusual because an axe was found wedged into the lid of the coffin, presumably to prevent the witch from returning after death. – AFP

Reading the morning's paper, the archaeologist in charge of the excavation feels doubly pleased. This is his doing, his find. Only yesterday, he made arrangements for the site to be guarded from unauthorised persons, to prevent vandalism, while he waits for radiocarbon dating and, if possible, DNA. He hopes these will confirm his theories.

It has been a coup for the department. Imagine the chances of finding a skeleton with that head? And the axe. Most graves tell little about the occupant, who they were. Sex and age are all you can hope for, usually, unless clothing or grave items give them away. But this coffin, so far from the nearest village, with the blade still in place. 'It's amazing,' he chuckles. 'This will secure me the chair, for sure.'

He is still whistling with satisfaction, when he locks up for the day and heads for the car park.

Next morning, he is back early, hoping for a call from the lab. But on opening his door, he is surprised to find on his desk, a letter, in an unknown hand. As he sips his coffee he reads.

To the Archaeologist
So, you think yourself clever to have found me thus. Now you sit in judgement, claiming to know me.

Yet, what can you know? The colour of my eyes? My hair?

What is it you say of me? That I was a witch? So be it. The world must have its goats to sacrifice and witches to know their place.

God knows I had enemies enough in the village, but there had been talk abroad of Dominicans, who would come scouring the land, seeking us out. Father Sprenger from Bâle and Father Krämer of Cologne.

I lived in fear of the day they would swoop down on our village, like great, white birds of prey, in their flowing habits, their black, mantle wings set to smother me.

Do you know Father Sprenger? Father Krämer? It was their Hammer of the Witches that gave the code, the guide by which to hunt us. Travelling far and wide, they searched every town and village.

For those who copulate with Devils.

Those who can Sway the Minds of Men to Love or Hatred.

Those who can Hebetate the Powers of Generation or Obstruct the Venereal Act.

Yet they professed themselves men of God. As if the Great Spirit himself had told them to seek out and destroy.

Those who could create a Prestidigitatory Illusion so that the Male Organ appears to be entirely removed and separate from the Body.

I speak truth when I say I knew none such.

So, tell me, who it was wielded the axe in a sign of power? Who it was wedged the blade into my coffin to ward off evil and prevent my return?

Ah! That you cannot tell.

Little did they know, those fools in the village, Death came to me like a lover. Taking me in his arms till I rejoiced in him.

Now, tell what conclusions you have drawn? That my teeth were bad? No worse than those of most in the village. The water we drank was bad, the food, oft-times worse.

Had I the ague, perhaps? A club foot? Bones stunted and crippled from years of pain?

Yet you cannot guess the colour of my hair. Was it a copper sheen, flowing over my shoulders in the warm light of the candle? Or sleek and black, glossy as ravens' wings?

Nor could you know the mark upon my neck, placed by the Devil himself, they said. Nor the secret nipple hid beneath my arm? From this, they claimed I fed my succubi, lizards and snakes I fondly kept in cages.

And my head, why was it shaped thus? You could not know I came born before my time, ripped from my mother's womb in the moment of her death. Nor that my brows were low and heavy, my head inclined to flattish.

The old women of the village told my father I would not live to see the dawn. I was a monster, deformed, proof the Lord of the Forest had coupled with my mother whore. Yet I survived.

They said I was brought into the world to do the Devil's mischief and bade my father take me to the darkest glade in the forest, to leave me there for wolves to devour.

But he would have none of it and sent them away.

Then, as time passed, he wreaked his own revenge, calling me child of Satan, my mother's murderess, raining blows upon my head and body that left me scarred and full of bile.

In the village, they began to call me Devil's progeny and cursed and spat on me as they passed, while others made to sign the Cross. Few there were to recognise the marks upon my face as those of man. Those that did, kept their silence, as though from secrets shared.

When I was full grown, there was none would take me willingly to wife, neither close at hand nor from villages across the mountains, so when my father died, I lived alone, inured to the taunts of those around me.

Yet, some still sought me out. Women in need of help. A salve to soothe a wound, a balm for faces thick with bruising, bodies reddened with welts. Not openly, but when their men did work in the fields, or roam the forests seeking wood, and game. Never the old women, those who pointed fingers first.

And from then on, should a white cat be born, or crops fail, or a milch cow run dry, I would hear them whisper against me. Then on the morrow I would find my cottage daubed with black and hateful signs.

I would know then it was time to bring in the chickens and the she goat and bar the door against them. Only in the dim light of the cottage would I be safe. There I would stay with my three-coloured cat, she with the double claws, my green-eyed lizards and smooth-skinned frogs. From their baskets, I took coils of sleepy snakes to place within the beds of those infirm to bring about a cure.

True, there were some that screamed and cried out when they woke to find their bedfellow, but I knew it to be the sound of sickness leaving their bodies. Some, indeed, parted with their senses, and the old women were quick to claim this proof of my powers, declaring then I was possessed of the evil eye.

Others swore by the scarlet flannel I wrapped around their loins to cure lumbago, or tight about their joints for rheumatism. I and my leeches knew the true colour of blood and its worth. As for those bleeding from the nose, was it not true that a skein of scarlet silk tied about the neck and knotted in front nine times would often staunch the flow?

Now, come, admit you cannot tell all that from my bones. So, what can you say of me?

Some women called for me, whenever the silver crescent moon rose high and they were brought to bed. And I would place around their necks a sigil charm, a ram's horn filled with fennel, or else a locket smooth of polished stone. I made certain that nothing be tied with knotted string, for if such be found, a child cannot be born aright.

Once, a woman came seeking relief from her belly. Sick she was, and afraid, this being her thirteenth, an uneasy number, and she with nothing to put in its mouth thereafter. So I mixed wormwood and mouse-ear, mandrake and motherwort and gave it her, and she went away, relieved of it, and the child lost.

Soon others heard and came seeking help, for the winter was proving long and hard, with many mouths to feed and little bread to fill them. Come the end of summer, with no babies born, the old women looked to me and cursed, as now you look upon my bones and speak.

Others, too, came seeking remedies, strong enough to curb a husband's lust. And true, I gave them powder, fine and white, made of the bitterest almonds, and told them to sprinkle it on the bread they served, but not to eat of it themselves, nor feed it to their children, but keep one loaf untouched and pure.

Soon the men fell sick with it, their faces bloodless, eyes all wild

53

and staring as they died in haste and the church bell tolled and would not leave off ringing.

At last, the old women began to talk among themselves, no longer in whispers when I passed, till I was afraid to leave my cottage, but at night. Only when all the village was asleep would I anoint myself with unguents, ointments of excrement, soot, cinqufoil and belladonna, aconite and water, hemlock and the pale, pale blood of poppies. Then I would fly, high above the village and look down on those my accusers sleeping soundly in their beds, neither straight, nor honest. Those that would attack a woman alone in the world, who then must fend for herself.

I would fly to the top of the ash tree that grew on the edge of the village there to converse with spirits. The ash, the father of trees, has the guardian spirits locked within its bark that have the power to take sickness away. I asked that they take from the village the sickness infesting it, that I may be left in peace.

Yet it was not to be. For when I returned to my cottage at daybreak, an owl, its eyes hooded from a night's full hunting, awaited me. Then I knew I was not long for this world, for to see an owl from the faery world is to see a shadow of one's own death.

At length came a crowd of men with torches towards the cottage, bent to burn it down, but the spirits of the tree let me see them coming, and so I fled deep into the forest.

Then came the tramp of boots, closer and closer, till I took from the placket deep within the folds of my skirt, one final draught, made of the harshest, bitterest of herbs. Monkshood and lavender, hemlock and meadow saffron. I lay down beside a stream with only the scarlet carp to watch me swallow.

How it burned and tore my throat as it did its lethal work, and thus I escaped.

Yet you cannot know these things.

Nor could you know that, having found me, they carried me back to the village, laid me on the church steps for all to jeer at. And while some women laughed, there were others standing silent, heads bowed, their fearful children clinging to their skirts.

Then the men did set about to shave my head, binding it fast with iron bands lest my spirit fly forth at night to roam abroad and cause more mischief.

One whole day they left me there, and one whole night, while the storks in their nests on the church steeple looked down in pity on me. The rooks in the trees cried out in sorrow wails and a thin, grey wolf came out of the forest to howl.

And on the third day the villagers ripped the metal bands from off my head and threw my body in a coffin, planed, of unmarked wood, and sealed it shut with many nails.

You say you have unearthed me, true, but what have you gleaned from me? That I was a witch? Perhaps. But let me ask you this, who was it struck the blow? Who held the axe? The lowest in the village? He? Not so.

Listen. For they carried me away from the village, far beyond the fields, up into the wildest part of the hills with only the wolves and eagles to bear me company. There, they said, my curse could not be felt.

Then with the wind tugging at his robes, the priest took up the axe and struck a mighty blow in the coffin lid. A sacred blow, he claimed, as the blade wedged hard, the wood shattered and a thousand tiny splinters fell about my face.

They said that be the end of me, but little did they know that in death I still could laugh at them. For having laid me on my back, as the axe fell, I turned my head and thus escaped the blow.

For did you not find me lying on my side?

You claim to know me, yet you cannot guess the colour of my eyes. Were they black? Small and bright, that glowed red in the dim light of the cottage? Or pale, a tawny gold, like the topaz eyes of a goat, to whom our hornèd Lord gave his own eyes when God was left with none after creating the beasts of the field?

It is not your place to presume, lest, in doing so, you may presume too much.

The archaeologist sits back, and stares at the letter, finally pushing it away in disgust. 'Some student prank obviously, and in poor taste. It can't be someone from the department, surely? No one would want the chair that badly?'

When the lab tests arrive confirming his dates, he finds little pleasure in them. He feels strangely flat, a little rattled, and tells his assistant he is off colour. That night, he heats up leftovers only to push the plate aside. His head aches, and his joints, he feels shivery. 'I must be coming down with something. Flu, probably. I've been pushing myself too hard.'

He gives up trying to read, switches off the lamp, and lies staring at the ceiling. 'Who would do such a thing? It's as if someone is trying to destroy me.'

Finally, in the cold, pale hour before dawn, his breathing grows heavier, and slowly he drifts into sleep, only to be suddenly, rigidly awake, as the thin, cold slither of a snake crosses his neck.

Strays

Gary lopes in, sighs and flops on the couch, a muddy grey jumper complementing his sheepdog fringe.

'Hi!' It could be a non-committal bark.

Edgar closes the door quickly. He could say, *What a surprise! Good to see you, Gary.* But doesn't.

Gary has a habit of loping in unexpectedly, picking up the morning's paper as if he's been out of the world for a month, consuming croissants, éclairs, petit fours, anything going, often lunch. Edgar is used to him. *He probably has a crush on me and, besides, one can hardly abandon the poor mutt on the doorstep.*

But Edgar's friends are beginning to wonder, 'Is this your latest?'

'No, of course not,' he insists. 'Merely an acquaintance. He lives nearby and drops in from time to time. Unannounced.' Edgar has assumed his personal life to be outside Gary's ken.

Edgar plans a dinner party for his oldest and closest friends and Gary turns up uninvited at seven twenty-five p.m.

'Gary, I'm awfully sorry, but I have friends coming for dinner.'

'That's all right, Ed. Don't mind me. I won't get in the way.' He moves down the hall, sweeps into the kitchen and is about to wolf down the vol-au-vents when Edgar whisks them out of reach.

He's like a stray starving for scraps. No family, obviously. The dear boy infuriates me but, God knows, he may be all I have one day!

So Edgar adds another place at the table and Gary joins the party. It is immediately apparent to Edgar's friends that Gary is out on a limb. Permanently.

'The only straight twig among us,' quips Charles.

'You must be a landscape gardener.' says Gary.

Charles purses his smile into something more serious, while Edgar glares at them both. 'Let's just say he's fond of *rare* blooms.'

'Oh, I see,' says Gary. 'Hot house stuff. Like orchids.'

Edgar is already regretting he has allowed Gary to stay. *He's like a Newfoundland dog shaking water over everyone*, and he decides to ignore him, 'So, Charles, how was the holiday?'

'Paradiso.' Charles reaches out and places a hand over Mario's. 'We spent most of the time with hardly a hibiscus between us, didn't we, darling?'

Mario's smile is beatifically coy.

'And the black boys?' Edgar wants to know.

'Black boys? You mean them grass trees?' Gary whispers, aloud.

Charles traps a laugh with his napkin as Mario smiles. Almost with affection.

Some time later, after the guests have left, Gary says, 'You've got some interesting mates, Ed. All in the plant business, are they?'

'In a manner of speaking.' Edgar yawns dramatically. 'Look, Gary, I really am most dreadfully tired.'

'Oh, you go to bed. Don't mind me. I can see meself out.'

Edgar groans and retires instead to the kitchen to start washing up. He is about to call Gary to help when he remembers he is already short of long-stemmed glasses.

Gary sits reading the paper. Then, when he has finished, he calls out, 'Thanks for the tea, Edgar. I had a real good time.'

Edgar winces as the door slams.

The following month, Edgar's job takes him to Adelaide. When he returns, there, on the doorstep, as if he hasn't moved the whole time, is Gary. *I'm surprised he isn't curled up on the mat, asleep.*

'Hi, Ed. Where've you been?'

'Adelaide, on business.' Edgar does not mention that business was interspersed with pleasure, nor that his new lover is arriving at the weekend. Instead, he says, 'I've been very busy and I have a simply frantic week ahead.'

Gary nods. *He can't be panting?* But after reading the paper, Gary leaves.

By Saturday, the house is spotless. A tub of orchids adorns the sideboard, a scarlet cyclamen graces the coffee table. When the doorbell rings, Edgar rushes to answer it.

'Darling!'

'Only me.' Gary bounds in and leaps on the couch, fringe flopping over his eyes.

'Bugger!' mutters Edgar. 'Gary, this really is most inconvenient. I'm expecting someone any moment and he'll only be here for the weekend *and* I have people coming for dinner.'

'Charles and Mario? Well, give 'em my best. I just popped round to tell you about me new flat. Over the shops. You can come and have a butcher's at it if you want. Get it?' he grins, hoping Edgar will too.

But Edgar is far from amused.

'One of your mates coming?'

'No.' Edgar tries bluntness. 'My new lover. if you must know. From Adelaide…so…'

'Oh, I won't get in the way.'

At that moment, the doorbell rings and Edgar is a long time answering. Eventually he returns, his face radiant, to announce, 'This is the *beautiful* Robert.'

The latter has been given a whispered explanation and smiles warmly as he shakes hands.

'Glad to meet you, Bob. I'm Gary. I expect Ed's told you all about me.'

Edgar suppresses a tiny cough.

'Are you in the plant business too?'

'No, I'm a public servant.'

'Gee, that's nice.'

Edgar sighs and gestures them to sit, offers coffee, adding sternly, 'One for the road, Gary.'

When they've finished, he takes the cups to the kitchen and decides, *Drastic measures.* 'Come!' he takes Robert by the hand, mouthing *Go!* at Gary as he passes.

The door of the bedroom closes, followed by muffled whispers.

Gary continues working his way through the papers, becoming engrossed in the history page. He is still reading as he stands and heads towards the bedroom. 'Hey!' Opening the door, he bounds in, 'There's this king had a tunnel from his bedroom to the queen's and another along the corridor to his girlfriend's... Gees, he must have been energetic.'

Edgar and Robert, in suspended animation, pull the sheet up to their chins and look *au fait. Please God, he doesn't leap on the bed and lick our faces!*

But Gary sits on the bed and continues reading in silence. Edgar and Robert remain where they are, wondering who should do what, and to whom.

'You two carry on, don't mind me,' says Gary.

Edgar feels a growing desire to murder him, so long as he can make it slow and painful.

Gary reads through the sport, comics, gardening and cookery sections, handy hints and, finally, classifieds.

For Edgar and Robert, the moment has gone. Desire abated, they climb out of bed and dress. They go into the kitchen for a brandy. Two, in fact. *God knows I need them.*

Before long, Gary barges in, 'I've finished the paper, Ed, so I'll be off. Real nice meeting you, Bob.' At the front door, he calls out, 'Thanks for the coffee.'

Edgar almost says 'Pleasure', but stops himself and the door slams.

It is a month before Gary reappears and when he does he is sporting a new look. *He's been to a canine beauty parlour*, Edgar decides.

'Bob here?'

'No.' Edgar's manner has chilled to zero.

'Nice bloke.' Gary pauses as if there is something else. 'Notice anything?'

Edgar studies him. *You're parading at Crofts?* 'You've…had your hair clipped, er – trimmed.'

'How'd you guess? And I've got a new jumper.'

A bone too? 'So I see. Grey and white suits you.'

'I'm in love, that's why.'

'Oh?'

'Yes. She knitted it for me.'

'Well, love works wonders. If given a chance.'

'It's that girl in the butcher's shop. Right under me nose, she was. Every time I bought me chops and sausages, she'd smile at me. Didn't take me long to realise I were in love. Funny, though, I never thought about it much till that day you had Bob here.'

'Indeed? Edgar arches an eyebrow.'

'Yeah, it was that article about the king having such fun that did it. And you and Bob, of course.'

'Really?'

'And I got to thinking it was high time I had someone special too. Her name's Sharlene. She's soft and warm and…'

Fluffy? Edgar is tempted but instead says, 'How clever of you!'

'I wanted you to be the first to know – man to man, like.'

'Quite.'

'She's coming round to me flat next weekend for a bit of – you know.' His elbow smashes meaningfully into Edgar's ribs.

Edgar coughs behind the thinnest of smiles and says, 'Good. Then I shall drop round with a lengthy novel.'

Sharlene moves in with Gary, who now has a warm bed and regular meals, so he no longer needs to turn up on Edgar''s doorstep, looking for scraps.

Robert resigns his job and moves east to be with Edgar, who is elated. Love like this has not happened to him in a long time and his spirits soar in the sunshine of the younger man's smiles. But the affair is short-lived. The eastern seaboard offers too many opportunities and Robert soon moves on to sample some other delights.

Edgar is devastated and braces as if for a funeral, brushing and ironing his darkest suits for work, lethargy his grey and constant companion. Apart from the office, he barely leaves the house, too flat to drag himself from this sudden slough.

Charles and Mario try everything. Parties, dinners, Charles even suggests a night's cruising, but Edgar cannot bear the thought and stays at home, steeping himself in Albinoni and gin.

Gary hears of the break- up and leaves a jar of Sharlene's tomato relish on the doorstep with a note: *Thought you might like something to cheer you up. Sharlene's a real little homemaker. Be seeing you. Keep your tail wagging, Gary.*

Edgar tries for a smile. *I wonder if her next trick will be to throw a litter?*

It is six months before Edgar decides to continue with life. No sooner does he venture forth than he meets Tim. Beautiful, sensitive. A student. The patches in his jeans aren't merely fashion. *I could do so much for the boy if only he will let me.*

He starts by taking him to dinner. At a good, but intimate little restaurant, hoping the evening will be a success and perhaps lead to other things. Tim seems cautious, wary, even.

When they arrive, Edgar is surprised to see Gary. A scrubbed-up, trimmed-down Gary, in white shirt and black trousers, albeit with brown suede shoes.

Edgar is momentarily distracted. *Oh, of course, Hush Puppies.*

'Hi, Ed. You didn't know I'd got meself a job as a waiter. It's my first week.' He leans closer. 'But don't worry. I'll do you proud. Put you at one of my tables. You might even give me a tip, eh?'

Edgar remembers this time to avoid Gary's elbow. He is determined not to allow him to spoil the evening and automatically hands over his lighter when Gary whispers that he's forgotten to bring one for lighting the candles. He even maintains his poise when Gary opens the wine with a *nonpareil* sprinkling of cork in the glass and grits his teeth when Gary delivers the wrong order. But when Gary drops a quail on the tablecloth, Edgar can barely control himself from punching him.

'Gee, I'm so sorry, Ed.'

At that moment, Tim laughs. Tension is released like doves of peace, and Edgar detects a certain change in ambience. He starts to make plans. Perhaps book tickets for a show and then supper? Arrange to meet Tim for coffee one weekend and take him shopping for clothes? Next week, have Charles and Mario over for dinner to meet him?

Tim looks at Edgar and smiles. Gary bounds round mopping the tablecloth and Edgar's shirtfront. Edgar sighs.

Then when Tim goes to the Gents, Gary whispers, 'Tim's real nice, Ed. You should hang on to him. And there's something I've been meaning to tell you. Me and Sharlene are getting married! I was thinking of asking you to be me best man, but now that I've seen you two, we could maybe have a double wedding! What do you say?'

Special Wording

'It was only a patch at first. A sort of whiskery growth. Like lichen. Small and on his chin.'

She is stuffing zucchinis into a plastic bag. Bending them into submission.

'I very nearly reached over and wiped it off. As you do. Only he doesn't like you drawing attention to his appearance. Razor nicks. Flecks of shaving foam. That sort of thing. And he never would use an electric.'

The last zucchini snaps in two but she shoves it in, regardless.

'Then I realised it was newsprint. Right there, a little patch of antimony staring me in the face, so I couldn't take my eyes off it. But when I went to read the words, they were too tiny. Even with reading glasses. Still, to me it looked like a snippet of *The Fin. Review.*'

She moves on to potatoes. Tubers and tap roots. Parsnips. Kumera. Swedes. Taro. Staple starches. She stands running her hand over the smooth skins of Desirées, ovals, pale as flesh, comparing them to Kipflers and Pontiacs before ripping off another bag to harvest them.

'Well, I said nothing, of course. I put it down to recent stress, overwork, long hours, and I felt sure that once he'd finished the big job he was working on, it'd go away. Overnight, hopefully. The lines around his eyes would disappear, leaving his face smooth as a baby's bottom. Almost.'

She passes the plump pumpkins. Butternuts and Queensland Blues. Green and golden gourds, spotted and knobbly, textured like desert lizards, before leaning over towards the parsnip patch. She begins dropping them heavy end first into a new bag, leaving the skinny ends sticking out, like long, thin feet from a bed.

'There are so many fancy veg you can choose from nowadays. Bok choy, okra, radiccio. Amazing. When I was a girl, we'd only just heard of avocados.'

On past the variegated greens of broccoli and fennel, mounds of pretty little Brussels sprouts, elegant French beans, decidedly proper English spinach, rocket, light enough to take off and darkly, sinister silver beet.

'Anyway, it was there again next morning, the spot, so I waited for him to say something about it. Surely, he must have seen it, shaving? Or else somebody at the office must have noticed and commented. Only they hadn't, it seems. Perhaps they were just too polite? Either that, or he wasn't saying.

'Then a couple of days later, I noticed a new patch. This time on his forehead, about five centimetres above his left eyebrow. Another dollop of *The Fin. Review*. I remember thinking that'll put the kibosh on it when you go to raise your eyebrow. How are you going to manage that quizzical look of yours? You won't be able to, not without a struggle.

'Then I thought perhaps I should tell him. Even if he didn't want to hear it. Better than leaving him ignorant. So I plucked up the courage, and said, "How was your shave this morning?" Casually. He gave me the Look. Or tried to, because the newsprint crinkled just as I'd thought it would and he looked as if he were pushing an ink blot up his face.

'"Fine," he said. Then, "Why?"

'So I knew he couldn't have noticed. Unless – and that's when it occurred to me, if he couldn't see anything different about his face, and the people in the office couldn't, then maybe I was only one who could and it set me thinking. Either I was going barmy in a hurry, or else I'd suddenly developed some amazing extrasensory, psychic, sixth sense.

'So I began scrutinising other people in shops and in the street, and on buses and trains to see if they were growing newspaper patches, too. But none of them were. Then I started wondering what could have caused it and decided it must mean he'd read far too many newspapers, over the years, and he'd developed some sort of allergy.'

She reaches the cucumber section – piled high with edible greens – 40 Reasons Why Cucumbers Are Better Than Men, supposedly. Big chunky normals, Telegraphs in tight-fitting, slinky, plastic spacesuits, and small, firm, hand-sized Lebanese.

'Then I thought, maybe, some alien was trying to send me a message from beyond. Like a medium. Only instead of holding hands with a glass tapping around a table, this was all coming out of him in a sort of daily bulletin, and perhaps I should start reading it.

'So I leant over and said, "Hold still a minute," and peered at his chin and forehead. It didn't make sense…*the jobless rate, which rose from 6.3 per cent*…was stuck to his chin, while…*prices have declined considerably in line with falling world oil prices*…was hovering above his eyebrow. What did that have to do with me?

'Fancy. All those years of propping the newspaper up over breakfast; him behind a paper wall, occasionally extending a hand to reach for his coffee and this was the result. Well, maybe it's a phase you're going through, and at the weekend, it'll disappear, Let's hope it's only a mid-week thing. Like a news flash.

'I dreaded the thought of the Saturday morning, and the weekend papers to wade through. At first, I hardly dared look at his face, fearing the worst, but then I took a quick peek over the colour supplement. There it was, another patch! On his cheek this time. And nothing financial. Sport. Well, it was the weekend, I suppose. I could tell it was sport. It was a bit of photo that looked like a footballer's bum, or part thereof. Caught in a ruck, I'd say, or wherever else footballers get caught.

'I felt relieved, somehow. If he was going to be covered in newsprint, there might as well be some variety. It made for a better layout. Pictures, as well as copy; news and current affairs, sport, entertainment, book reviews, theatre, tiny pars of human interest, maybe even cookery sections. A spread like that could last me till Monday.

'It was much better. I found myself looking at him with renewed interest. He was not only keeping abreast of the news, he was on top of it. His headlines were up to date. In fact, he'd become a walking news stand.

'There, in front of me, new patches had appeared, the results of last week's race meetings at Randwick, Doomben, Moonee Valley and Sandown. Not to mention the midweek, snap-happy Dapto Dogs meeting. And without my even having to open the paper!

'I could find out details of the latest Audi 8, if I wanted to, or even buy a second-hand Mitsubishi Pajero Exceed, if I felt so inclined. I could read up on the proposed new owners of Virgin and find out who was talking to whom in the Libs.

'That was when I got up and made a strong pot of tea. This was going to need concentration. And stamina, if I was to read him right. Especially since I'd spotted one of those tiny little headlines tucked away at the side of his cheek, near his left ear: *Balcony sitter was dead STOCK-HOLM: An elderly woman sat for two months on her balcony before a neighbour discovered she was dead, it was reported yesterday. The 84-year-old woman might have died while watching fireworks from her apartment on New Year's Eve, police said. The woman was found sitting on a chair on her balcony, dressed in a coat and hat.*

'How terrible! And there was another, just below his right ear: *Dead baby LONDON: A woman who died aged 92 had been carrying her dead baby – long since calcified – for 60 years, two Austrian doctors reported yesterday.*

'How sad! Only by this time I'd moved on to the real estate supplement and was trying to figure out where our suburb fitted in to the top price areas for recent house sales. It didn't, apparently. And as for the job section, who was going to employ me as a crane driver, which was the only thing that appealed to me? Whatever happened to good old-fashioned occupations, like cordwainer, dogger, aleconner, or beggar-banger? Just for argument's sake, suppose I wanted to be a plumassier, lattener, jarvey or tambourer? I'd be hard-pressed to find anything on offer.

'Naturally, after that, I kept a close eye on him, and gradually I let him become my mine of information. Other papers started to appear, too. Tabloids, as well as broadsides. On Sundays and Mondays, there were TV guides, intermingled with the week's Stars, and later on, bits of *The Bulletin* and *National Geographic* started to pop up. In the end, I was able to cancel the normal paper delivery – there was no need for it. I had him all to myself and could read him like a book.

'Of course, I tried to do something about it. As his wife, I felt a responsibility. So I took to standing behind him in the bathroom, saying, "Hang on a minute," and I'd wipe his neck with a tissue, or, "Wait, there's a bit you've missed here." Then I'd grab a face washer and start scrubbing, only have you ever noticed how hard antimony is to get off, once it's embedded in the skin? I tried a sponge, then a squeegee and even once a bit of steel wool (soap impregnated, of course) but even that didn't work. "Ouch, that hurt!" was all he said, and he thumped me, so I gave up the thought of trying a blow torch.

'Sometimes I had to ask him to turn a little this way or that, like turning a page, because it was hard to read him at an angle, but mostly it was fine, even though it was only ever bits and pieces of articles, never a full page. And as you'd expect, each day his news content changed.'

She reaches the fruit section. Strawberries, mangoes, guavas and persimmons. She fondles them lovingly. Feijoas, raspberries, peaches and tamarillos. Smooth to the touch of a finger. Soft as skin.

'It didn't stop there, either. There were fragments of words turning up on his back like scribbly black moles that needed watching. Then it started to leach out over his armchair and across the rug, which was a bit much. There were odd spots of lettering on cushions and the lampshade, and, as for his side of the bed, it was truly black and white and read all over. The print column started inching its way up the walls and no matter what laundry detergent or household spray I tried, it simply wouldn't come out.

'Once, I even decided it was like a jigsaw. Odd bits were missing and I found myself wanting to fill in the gaps.

'Then, one day I decided to fight fire with fire, so to speak. I went to the recycle bin for some old newspapers. I sat in a sunny spot in the garden and tore them into thousands of tiny pieces. After that, I made up a big pot of glue on the stove, flour and water based, tossing in a bit of wallpaper glue I found at the back of a cupboard. When it was cool, I waited till his attention was distracted then began pasting tiny pieces of newsprint over the gaps to make him all smooth.'

She holds up a big bunch of grapes, admires the weight and fullness. Lovingly strokes the furred skin of kiwis, ruffles the curly haired lychees, before moving on again.

'Papier mâché, it was. Layer upon layer, to form a skin. Well, it took me weeks – I had to let each coat dry before starting on the next. But, finally, once the layers were thick enough, I removed the head and cut down the middle, then scooped out the pulp, like passionfruit seeds, and threw it away. Then I taped the sides back together and stuck a cardboard cylinder up the centre for a handle.

'You see, I'd made myself a puppet, one I could actually talk to, who wouldn't answer back, or disagree, or say anything untoward or grumpy. Quite the contrary. I christened him A for Acquiescence.'

She'd reaches the checkout and empties her trolley of artichokes, aubergines, capsicums and corn, parsnips and pomegranates, mushrooms and mung beans, finishing up with yams and zucchinis.

'When I'd finished, I noticed quite by accident six patches of newsprint in a row, riding roughshod over his nose in a kind of pattern:

finance current affairs real estate sport

'It seemed a mantra of sorts, that rather suited him.'

She pays the girl and puts the change into her purse.

'Well, I suppose you're wondering what I did with him? Truth is, there was nothing I could do. I thought of lighting a fire down the bottom of the yard and burning off some tree prunings at the same time, only it's not ecologically friendly. Burning off, that is. I don't have a fuel stove and it would never have done to put him in the compost.

'So in the end I just bundled him up and put him out with the paper recycling, along with the rest of his *Fin Reviews*. That seemed the best thing, really, and I knew he's be happy there.'

Figure 8

She remembered standing at the window looking out to sea when she saw the whale. It sent up a spray as if in greeting, but when she told Cynthia, all she said was, 'Nonsense, Mum. It was probably light playing on the sprinkler and you blinked.'

But she saw it. Gliding through the water, dipping and rolling, belly up, diving again, tail up then *THWAP!* Down on the water. It was 8 August. My wedding anniversary, that's how I remembered. *It seemed as if it had no particular plans that day and had only come into the harbour for a break. A splash and a swim to celebrate the last of winter.*

Of course Cynthia didn't believe me. Claimed it was another of my 'little turns'. How I hate that expression. Reminds me of those silly pirouettes kids used to do. All rag curls and tutus, play acting for grown-ups. Next door's kids were the worst and Cynthia was always trying to ape them.

Haha! Ape them. Blue-bottomed apes. Presenting.

There had been a whale, hadn't there?

On Monday morning, the doorbell rang.

'Oh, you like my number, do you? Yes, I'm fond of it too. Opal chips. Pretty, aren't they? It was here when I came. The last resident must have put it there. I wonder would you mind putting the meal on the table? I find it difficult to manage it on the walker. Thank you so much.'

She saw the woman to the door.

'Eight has always been my lucky number. I was born on the eighth, married on the eighth too. Sheer coincidence, of course, but as a child I used to think it was such a sad number. Like two sad eyes on top of each other, looking up at you.

'I've been here seventeen years next month. We found it cramped at first and my husband missed his garden. There's no gardening to do here, it's all done for you, so he went downhill. I coped for as long as I could, but in the end, they had to move him to the nursing wing because by then I couldn't lift him. Probably just as well. There's no way I could have managed now, not on a frame.

'Not too bad, thank you. My eyesight's not what it was, of course, and my hearing's almost gone, but I hang in there. But I do find it hard to cook these days. Don't know what I'd do without Meals-on-Wheels. Packet soup, I expect. Oh dear, not curried prawns? I do hope they're all right? One can never be too careful, you know. And I don't want the trots all night. What's for pudding? I like pudding. Cake. Not again? I can't stand cake. They know that. I've told them often enough. If it's cake, throw it out, because I won't eat it. I've told them to send fruit, but there's no chance of that, I suppose. Still you'd think they could manage a jelly, at least.

'I expect they'll be wanting to put me in the nursing wing next and give my unit to someone else. They say there's a waiting list. But I won't go. Not without a fight. I used to say when my time was up, I'd head off into the Simpson desert with a bottle of champagne. Metaphorically speaking. I don't drink. Well, maybe a couple of small sherries at night. Cynthia says I'd need at least two bottles of champagne. But I'll think of something. A plastic bag over my head tied round the neck, maybe. Trouble is, sometimes I dream about it. That I've changed my mind and panic and I'm trying to breathe, clawing at the plastic and instead of going to sleep, I'm found by that awful woman next door looking an absolute shocker, plastic clinging to my face and skin all blue and blotchy. No, I'd prefer something with a bit of finesse. A dignified exit. Otherwise, what's the point? They may as well hit me over the head with a brick now.

'I don't trust sleeping pills. They're too much like anaesthetic. You have no control. Besides, my uncle died under chloroform. He took an afternoon nap on a sofa and lay on a darning needle. It went straight into his back, poor man, and broke into two pieces. One went down his leg, the other up his back. Dreadful way to go. It was before X-rays, so they just had to keep digging to find the pieces and in the end he died on the operating table.

'My husband? Oh, he had Parkinson's. Died in that building over there, the other side of the garden. I like to think he had a view before... Anyway, they came and told me it was time, that if I wanted to see him... But I was slow, so when I got there, it was too late. Not that it would have made much difference. He didn't know me by then.

'Of course, dear, you run along, mustn't let the other meals get cold. But I wonder, would you mind posting some letters for me? You noticed? Yes, to the prime minister. I've been wanting a word with him for some time. I'm not sure he knows what he's doing, poor thing. I thought it best to tell him. The other one? That's to the Pope. He could do with some advice as well. You're sure you don't mind? Thank you, that's so kind.

'Oh, don't look now, there's that hideous creature from next door. Pay no attention to her. She *claims* to have been in *Theatre* and we all know what that could mean! I wonder they let types like her into a place like this. Dead common, if you ask me. She never misses a trick. And nosy! Huh!

'What I'd really like to see me off is a little fire. Spontaneous Human Combustion they call it. Such a grand-sounding name. I've read all about it. It's when a person burns to death but there's no obvious source of fire. They used to call it Fire from Heaven. Divine. Sometimes it can be three thousand degrees Fahrenheit! *Wooosh!* Your whole body disintegrates completely till nothing's left but ash. Supposedly. Well, maybe a bit of clothing, but that's the odd thing about it. The clothing. There's often an item left. Like a black satin slip or stocking. And one would hope not something to create the wrong impression. I like to think of it as one's own little nuclear blast. Like the Turin shroud, or Saint Veronica's hanky, only without the face. Still, I mustn't ramble on. Oh wait! There's just one other letter. Would you mind? It's to Jesus Christ. I

73

have a few things I want to get off my chest, before… You did say you were going to the post office?'

Good gracious! This mirror's an absolute disgrace! Here you are standing here nattering and you didn't even notice how dirty your face was. And your lipstick's smudged to buggery. What would Next Door say?

Tuesday morning: 'My door number? Oh, you noticed. Yes, opal chips. I can't stand them myself. They're unlucky. That bitch next door put it up.'

Royal Command

'Gerry! It's me, Zak... You got a minute? Have I got the most *fabulous* script for you. In the Bible!... Yeah, I know de Mille's done it. But he was hung up on Moses, remember? This is different. It's de Mille does *Days of Our...* No, not the modern version, the funny old one. King John's? No, King James. But just wait till you read it! It's got everything – sex, greed, jealousy. You'll love it. Title? Haven't got one yet. The working title's *The Book of Esther.*'

Now it came to pass in the days of Ahasuerus...which reigned, from India even unto Ethiopia, over an hundred and seven and twenty provinces...

We cross now to the king's valet, Roger.

'King Ahasuerus? He's the one the Greeks, called Xerxes. You know, the Battle of Salamis – around 484 BC. Gorgeous butch thing. Long, dark, curly hair, and oh, that *beard!*

That in those days when the king Ahasuerus sat on the throne of his kingdom, which was in Shushan the palace...

'Now, just put the tables over there, will you, and set the bar up next to the pool. God, I hope it doesn't rain – I can't cope with muddy sandals all over the rugs.'

In the third year of his reign, he made a feast unto all his princes and his servants; the power of Persia and Media, the nobles and princes of the provinces, being before him...

'Now let's see. We'll pop the princes of Persia in the right wing, and the princes of Media in the left and let's just hope they all sort themselves out by breakfast.'

When he shewed the riches of his glorious kingdom and the honour of his excellent majesty...

'It's all conspicuous consumption, if you ask me. But he would insist on throwing a huge party. He just wanted to show off in front of those foreign princes. Cecil B has nothing on him!'

And when these days were expired, the king made a feast unto all the people that were present in Shushan the palace, both unto great and small, seven days, in the court of the garden of the king's palace...

'All that means is the kitchen staff got to take home leftovers and the gardeners got bottles of XXXX.'

Where were white, green, and blue, hangings, fastened with cords of fine linen and purple to silver rings and pillars of marble: the beds were of gold and silver, upon a pavement of red, and blue, and white, and black, marble...

'And in the end it did look fabulous, if I say so myself, but he gave me a free hand. The poor darling has no sense of style, he's all glitz and mirrors.'

And they gave them drink in vessels of gold...and royal wine in abundance, according to the state of the king...

'It was totally laid on of course and they all had too much to drink. Thankfully, no one had to drive home. Booze chariots were out in droves. Meanwhile, Madam the Queen was in her quarters entertaining the wives. And let's face it, the party was nothing more than a seven-day piss-up with the King right off his face, poor lamb. Quite green. And argumentative! When I suggested he have a Berocca and sleep it off, would he hear of it? Absolutely not! Talk about snappy! Instead, he sent for the court chamberlains.

To bring Vashti the Queen before the king with the crown royal, to shew the people and the princes her beauty for she was fair to look on...

'To each his own, I always say.'

But the Queen Vashti refused to come at the king's commandment by his chamberlains: therefore was the king very wroth, and his anger burned in him...

'And did that bring on a Royal Tizz! Shouting and carrying on a treat. Felt like putting him over my knee and giving him a good spanking. In front of the princes. I could have told him Madam would be difficult. She's never been the type to stick to running a palace and doing the flowers.'

What shall we do unto the Queen Vashti according to law, because she hath not performed the commandment of the King Ahasuerus by the chamberlains?

'Of course, had he been sober, the last thing he'd have wanted was her flouncing round with only a crown on her head. But by this time he was off his face. Pissed as a peacock. And after that, they all had their knives out, all scared their wives would do the same and refuse to obey. Women can be so militant when they choose.'

If it please the King, let there go a royal commandment from him, and let it be written among the laws of the Persians and the Medes, that it be not altered, That Vashti come no more before King Ahasuerus: and let the King give her royal estate unto another that is better than she...

'That's all there was to it, really. He was so smashed, he sent out the decree then and there and by the time he'd sobered up, it was too late. The papparazzi had got hold of it and it was front page news.'

'The phone wouldn't stop ringing. "Care to make a Royal statement? Can we have a few words, Sire? Just a minute of your time, Majesty?" When what they wanted was a Royal Decree in time for the afternoon edition. It was all over the placards.'

PALACE GAZETTE
ROYAL ROMANCE OR PALACE TAKE-OVER?
SHUSHAN DAILY
KING DUMPS OLD QUEEN FOR UNKNOWN
TIT-BIT
DAILY TRUTH
PALACE ROCKED BY ROYAL SEX SCANDAL!
PERVY PARTIES IN PRIVATE PARTS
JEWISH NEWS
NO COMMENT...ALREADY

The following is an extract from a journal found in the private apartments of the King, written in his own Royal hand.

Vashti was there again today. In that kiosk of hers and it's starting to get to me. I can't have her forcibly removed from the grounds. It would look bad and the kiosk is outside the palace gate, just. Besides, the press would have a field day.

She's completely changed. She wears awful black lipstick and her hair's dyed. Solid black. Why can't she just have it streaked, like most women her age?

I thought of charging her with sedition – I even had the secret police infiltrate the kiosk to find out what she was selling. But it was only lifesavers, postcards, condoms, that sort of thing. That's until she found out that Esther was a former Miss Israel and she added yarmulkes.

If she thought she'd win me over, she didn't. Esther wasn't the reason we split up. No. Vashti had become far too aggro. Refusing to come when I called. And in front of all those princes, too. She made me look such a fool. As if I could fight battles overseas but couldn't control my own wife.

Still, I suppose everyone changes with time. Even Esther's not quite the same. She's gone all ethnic on me and is into fund-raising in a big way. Kibbutzes, ambulances, universities, you name it, she'll raise the funds for it.

Not that I mind. It keeps her busy when I'm away at war. And besides, how could I refuse her? She's got legs up to her arm-pits and she's blonde. Actually, her hair's the most amazing honey gold and she assures me it's natural.

She gives great massages too and helps me in and out of my armour. She even answers my iPhone. She says power turns her on.

The trouble with Vashti was she never really understood me. She said I was obsessed with power. But that's not true. A king has to look good in front of his enemies. It's all PR but Esther says it's okay for me to express my feminine side, as well.

She makes me feel young and hot-blooded, calls me her 'stud'. Even has me dress differently. Says kaftans went out in the 70s and if you've got it, flaunt it.

Of course, my valet, Roger, had to go. She insisted. She ordered a new wardrobe for me. Tight jeans to show off my 'cute buns'. Open shirts. Gold chains.

I had thought for a while Vashti would come running back, but she didn't. She disappeared at first, then suddenly, there she was in that

damned kiosk, waving at me. I got such a shock, I almost pranged the
chariot.

Must stop, now. Esther's paging me and I don't like to keep her
waiting.

'Is that you, Gerry? It's me Zak. What do you think? Have we got us a
series?'

All Round the Room

They used to joke – which came first? Ollie or the village? The village was settled early, back when some prospector counted on finding gold in the creeks around. That proved a furphy. But how old Ollie was, nobody knew. They couldn't remember a time when she wasn't there. So the village, nestling like a pendant between warm, bosomy hills, and Ollie were seen as – old as each other, almost. A hundred and thirty, give or take.

She hailed from the Big Smoke, wherever that might be, and arrived with a husband in tow, looking for work. It was mostly timber back then, drawn by bullock dray and later, by jinker, but now it was dairying. He scarpered soon after, never to be heard of again and, with a few too many drinks downed, some of the locals would mutter that maybe she'd disposed of Mr Ollie and buried him down the bottom of the hill, or else cemented him in the hollow old tree behind her house. Not that rumours bothered Ollie. She merely smiled and shrugged, adding fire to smoke.

The village boasted a general store and butcher's, a pub, the boarding house, plus a dozen houses. Ollie started working in the boarding house, but later she came into a little money from an aunt, enough to buy one of the long-empty houses, a ramshackle old place in need of shoring up, not from white ants, just age. It's what happened to places where the timbers were arthritic. And there was a garden, big and overgrown with gnarled fruit trees, avocados and cherry guavas. Soon, Ollie was putting in rhubarb and all manner of vegies and herbs.

At first, the locals didn't take to her. Not that she wasn't polite enough – there was never a cross word or sliver of gossip from her – but she wasn't 'one of them'. Not born and bred. An outsider. And her house didn't help, either. Okay, it was hers to do as she liked, but she put half the village offside when she set about painting it herself, and at midday, when it was hottest. She said the paint would dry faster, but the blokes on the veranda of the pub were watching and they agreed one of them should have done it. They would have too, eventually. Better that than making a fool of herself with the brush tied to a broom handle to paint the bits she couldn't reach by ladder. And the colours! Downright offensive. They would have said, leave the galvo roof, paint the walls dirt-brown, and anything else beige. Not white, and definitely not that glossy black door and matching window frames, let alone a red roof that was going to frighten the cows for sure.

But the funny thing was, when they went home to their wives, they said why shouldn't she paint her house any colour she liked. Pink and grey like a galah, even, since she didn't have some man telling her what to do. Besides, if she'd waited for them to do it, she'd be waiting years.

So the women came to accept her before the men. They'd go walking with her looking for blackberries by the side of the road, or mushrooms in the fields after rain, when the rains weren't so heavy that the river rose, the bridge went under and they were cut off completely. But every day, over the hills and back down into the valley. Ollie was generous sharing her produce, too, avocados, oranges as many as she could reach, and plenty of parsley. Once, she gave a big bunch to a small child for its mother, only to have the older sister rush up moments later insisting Ollie take twenty cents.

'But I've plenty, really.'

'Mum says you must. If you give a woman parsley, she'll fall pregnant within a week and there's six of us already.' So Ollie took the twenty cents, wondering how many bunches of her parsley had increased the population in other houses.

In time, Ollie acquired a cat. The village regarded cats as working animals, to keep vermin at bay, they didn't need feeding. But to Ollie, Grimalkin was a companion.

'What did you say his name was?'

81

'Grimalkin. It's an archaic word meaning cat.'

Given local felines were only ever referred to as Cat, or Hey! Get-out-of-it, this seemed a bit fancy.

One pet cat was considered odd, but allowable, but when she added another, it became eccentric, especially when she named it Broomstick.

Then one of the neighbours found a litter under a rainwater tank, dead but for one which he was about to drown, when Ollie rushed up shouting, 'Stop! I'll take it!' and, when asked, said she'd be naming it Morgan le Fay. Why on earth would she call a cat that? He stood scratching his head as he watched her go.

Nor was that the last of it. When the neighbours either side started shooting at a feral cat, Ollie swore she'd heard a howl of pain and, al-though she didn't approve of feral cats per se, she thought it might have been injured and wanted to treat it. So she began placing a bowl of food on the back veranda each night trying to coax the animal in to catch it. But first the cat had to submit to a pat from Ollie before being fed.

All went well for a while, and Ollie thought the cat was getting the message about being, maybe not BFF, but friends at least, when one night she was watching something on TV and forgot about the cat. No sooner had she settled down than she felt herself glared at and there was the cat, at her feet, preparing to spring. Ollie shrieked and ran into the bedroom, the cat in pursuit. She jumped on the bed, the cat circling, hissing, threatening to attack, and Ollie desperate. What had gone wrong? Then she realised, she hadn't patted the animal. Very gingerly, she reached down to touch the cat's head, and instantly it raced out to the veranda and wolfed down its food.

Ollie hoped these pre-dinner pats might in time lead to stroking, then cuddling and the feral cat would eventually become tame enough to move in. Which is exactly what happened and when that day came, Ollie named her Halloween.

For the locals, this was completely unheard of. Nobody needed four cats, especially ones with funny names and even funnier habits. When-ever Ollie crossed the road, they would form into line, legs in unison, moving like the traction on a Sherman tank, following, she said so they could choose what they wanted for dinner.

No doubt about it, the locals shook their heads, Ollie might be tolerated, but she'd never be 'one of them'.

Then came Seniors' Week and the school decided to honour the village's elderly citizens by inviting them for morning tea. Songs were sung, after which came tea and scones in the hall, and Ollie, who'd joined them, felt it had been a success. Apart from the fact that all the other old ladies wore pastels, floral prints and cardies and she'd worn her only pair of black, town-going slacks and a black jacket, because she didn't own any pastels.

The following year, she was unable to attend Seniors' Week, because she'd broken a tooth and the dentist in the nearest town could only take her at that time. So she sent her apologies and thought no more about it. She was surprised, therefore, when she found a note in her letterbox written in a childish hand saying,

Dear Mrs Ollie
    Our teacher, Mr Jones, says you are an old lady who wears black and has four cats. Can you please tell us a spell?
    Thank you from
        Year 3

Ollie wasn't sure how to react. Had the teacher been discussing her with the children? Then she decided no, it was probably part of a creative writing class, meant to trigger their little imaginations, so she decided to respond in kind.

She took out her witch's missal, which she'd bought years before in a second-hand bookshop thinking it might come in useful some day and thumbed through till she found a sixteenth-century love charm:

Take a nutmeg and prick it full of holes and you shall see it wear a dew upon it. Put it in your armpit for two days, and then dry it upon a tilestone and so it will fall to powder, the which you put in the desired one's portion of potage or drink. Do not eat of it yourself. They shall love thee without doubt.

Having copied this in as flowery a hand as her arthritis could manage, she put it in an envelope, sealed and addressed it to Year 3, and popped it in the school letterbox one evening after sunset when no one would see her.

Next year's Seniors' Week, came another letter from a new Year 3:

Dear Mrs Ollie,
   Our teacher, Mr Jones, says you are really, really old and that you know a lot of spells. Could you please give us one.
      Yours cerncilly
         Year 3

This time, Ollie was greatly put out. How dare the teacher egg on the children in this way. Still, not wanting to appear a bad sport, she wrote,

To Make Oneself Invisible
Take five black beans and the head of a dead man...

She was hoping this would be enough to discourage the children, and she continued, ingredient after ingredient, which would normally have been followed by an incantation, but here she stopped because she didn't want to put the children at risk. They would have difficulty enough finding the ingredients and may even give up early, but some bolder children still might try giving voice to the spell, which included words aligned to the darker elements. So she wrote,

I have deliberately left some words out of the spell, because I don't want you conjuring up beings that could prove dangerous. If, however, an evil presence should suddenly manifest itself in the classroom, stop the spell IMMEDIATELY!

There, that should do it, she thought, but when Seniors' Week came round yet again and there was the usual letter, Ollie was more than annoyed. This time, she sent no spell, merely a letter saying,

Dear Class 3
   Please tell Mr Jones from me that it is not polite to pick on old

ladies who happen to wear black and own cats. I will not be sending any more spells.

    Signed
        Mrs Ollie

After that, there were no more letters, but the villagers, the blokes especially, regarded her as even more odd, 'Fancy treating the kiddies like that,' they muttered, and some even started avoiding her.

The children now became more polite, chorusing, 'Good afternoon, Mrs Ollie,' if they saw her in the main street, and the women still swapped produce with her.

She and her fellow walkers took to doing 'marathons' to the nearest town, thirty kilometres there, thirty back, raising money for charities, while the blokes offered to supervise from the pub veranda.

So life in the village continued much as before.

Then one of the local lads decided to get married and his mates organised a buck's party, which, according to village tradition, meant after being plied with several drinks, the groom would be taken into a remote part of the rainforest and lashed to a tree. Despite its lush beauty, the district was known as Yowie country, thickly populated with wild dogs, snakes and spiders. Moreover, it could be freezing and the victim was expecting a night involving all of the above when he spotted a rope sticking out the door of one of the cars and panicked. Without waiting, he took off, charging through the trees, before his mates realised he'd gone, only to arrive back at the village hours later, covered in mud, cuts and scratches, his clothes in tatters, ending up, short of breath on Ollie's back veranda.

Halloween, still vaguely feral, began hissing the alarm and Ollie went to see what the fuss was about. 'Oh dear, Bobby, you are a mess. You'd better come in.' She gave him a bowl of soup, cream for his cuts and scratches and an old tracksuit, left by her long-forgotten husband. 'I knew I'd find a use for it some day. Now don't go home tonight. They'll be out looking for you but they won't think to come here,' she chuckled.

So Bobby accepted a blanket and gratefully bedded down on her couch for the night and went home early next day.

Not long after this, Ollie began to suspect there was something seriously wrong with her. During the day, she felt not quite right but, come night, she was queasy with undetermined aches and pains, so she went to bed early, only to wake in the middle of the night convinced she was dying. She managed to stagger out of bed, find pen and paper and write a note to Bobby. In it she said she was calling in a favour, and could he please contact a cousin of hers in Sydney and ask her to come and take the cats. Then she went back to bed, and died.

Next morning when she didn't appear for her usual early walk, some of the women came to the house and found her lying peacefully in bed, with Grimalkin, Broomstick, Morgan le Fay and Halloween forming a catafalque on the corners.

The police and undertaker were called and some of the blokes downed a few stiff drinks before helping get the body out of the house and into the hearse. They almost panicked when they saw froth on her mouth, and she was surprisingly heavy. It was as much as they could do to manoeuvre the body into the hallway, but unfortunately, in doing so, Ollie's nightie was accidentally hoisted up and, as they turned to lower it discreetly, they saw her eyes openly glaring at them and they all but dropped her then and there.

The cousin from Sydney arrived for the funeral and as a mark of respect some of the locals turned up. Not all, but most. One said, somewhat uncharitably in the pub, 'Ollie won't be coming to my funeral, so why should I go to hers?' which seemed only fair, and the others agreed. But the women were there, and Mr Jones, the teacher, plus Bobby and the blokes who'd helped get her into the hearse.

They all agreed that Ollie, although not 'one of them', had been a fixture of sorts, and some of the blokes who'd been there at the end wished they'd been a little more respectful towards her in life. Because, sure as eggs, they'd be having nightmares now for years to come, what with the way her eyes had followed them all round the room.

Had As Leif Control

Letter from:
Earl Bathurst to Governor Darling.

Downing Street, 17 August, 1825.

Sir,

With reference to my Dispatch of the 22 July, 1824, to take measures for the reoccupation of Norfolk Island, to which place the worst description of Convicts might be sent. I transmit to you the copy of a letter by Major Morriset of the 48th Regt., whose experience in the management of Convicts points him out as a very fit person for the position. I strongly recommend the appointment of Major Morriset as Commandant to Norfolk Island, with such reasonable Salary as you may consider proper.

I have, &.,

BATHURST.

Emily has decided she will walk today, to the other side of the bay and back. It is a pleasant enough morning and there can be no harm, surely? After all, James has merely told her not to ride. She suspects he plans to take the horse himself, reduced as they are now, to one.

She shudders to think of the poor horses lost at sea, when the storm broke. The ship's hatches were battened down, but the horses were hurled against their stalls in the hold, bashed and injured, some killed, their bodies thrown overboard to feed the sharks.

It is such a pity not to be out riding when the weather promises to be pleasant, after days of rain. She was so looking forward to it. Riding has now become her particular pleasure; there is little else for her to do. She loves the feeling of being raised, the breeze in her face, as she makes her way down Military Row to the water's edge. There to sit motionless in the saddle, gazing out, hoping for the sight of a sail on the far horizon.

It means she must pass the gaol, with its long uneven walls of stone, broken only by the archway serving as gallows. She cannot help but shudder whenever she passes. James has said there are thirteen steps to the gibbet and she wonders, *Do the sad wretches that climb them ever count?*

It is now mid-morning and still cold on the veranda. Trees overhang the house, like a cloak, blocking out the morning sun, keeping it dark, enclosed. Secretive. By afternoon, it will creep up towards the eaves, spilling over the sills to the rooms beyond. Then, as dusk falls, the fires will be lit, dispelling the threat of shadows once more.

The servant, Turner, has cleaned and blackened the grates, stripped and made the bed. The doctor and some of the officers are expected to dine with them this evening. Emily has already given orders for more bread to be baked and the pork to be soaked. There is not much to work with and though she tries to work miracles with a little sage and parsley, she wonders if James ever notices her efforts.

Now, she opens her workbox and threads her needle, takes out her embroidery frame, only to lay it in her lap with a sigh. She has grown so weary of sewing, something that once gave so much pleasure. Now she merely aches for someone to talk to, other than a man. Someone to share her secrets, the little things, another woman.

Those last letters she had from home she has read many times over, folding and creasing the paper so often it has started to tear. She has deduced every shadow of meaning from the lines, the words unsaid, pictures conveyed, in the hope of seeking the truths lying behind.

Her sister's child is sickly pale still, and she wonders will it survive the damp of another Yorkshire winter? Her brother, in London, has acquired new friends who sound too wild and racy by far, and what of his drinking, his gaming debts? She knows him only too well and worries for him. As for her parents, no longer young, how do they fare? The letters barely hint at such matters.

Emily sits with her embroidery in her lap, staring out at the monotony of blue that skirts the island and feels herself a prisoner. Every bit as much as the beasts locked up at night without benefit of stars above them.

It is still not noon when she closes her workbox and goes into her bedroom. Taking off her morning gown, she steps into her day dress, pulling it up and buttoning the bodice. She exchanges silk slippers for neat leather boots, which she laces tightly.

Opening the door onto the veranda, she runs down the steps and heads for the tiny beach her husband, Major Morriset, has named Emily Bay for her. It is only a curve of sand, but if she closes one eye and looks beyond her outstretched arm, she can imagine it fitting within the palm of her hand.

She hears the squish of sand underfoot as she walks, feels it working its way through the eyelets of her boots, rubbing between her toes. She loves this feeling of grit. It makes her feel like a child again, untethered and free to play at will.

High above the island, looming cliffs are topped by a hairline of brooding pines, but here in her bay, the sand is pale, the bushes around her low and scrubby. She feels they offer a sense of peace that sets this place apart.

The sun is now high overhead as she sets out to walk the length of the sand to where the longboats tie up. Today there are no ships riding at anchor inside the reef and no small boats out fishing.

She can hear the waves as they break on the reef, only to crash against the rocks on the foreshore, sending spumes of spray high in the air, while up in the hills, the wind sighs wretchedly through the sombre pines.

Emily reaches the end of the beach, but makes no attempt to turn back, telling herself there are still hours before Turner will need to start cooking dinner. She can easily be back in time to change.

Then she hears the cry of an animal caught in a trap and is about to part the bushes and step through, when something pulls her back. A group of men, gathered around a prisoner, his arms manacled above his head, tied to a triangle. Legs apart, he stands, his cries floating back towards her as she stands rigid behind the bushes.

The man's back is already bloodied as a soldier steps forward and shoves a plug of leather between his teeth.

THWACK – she hears the lash comes down again and the overseer call, 'TEN!

The man's head jerks back, his back arching in spasm.

Between the leaves, Emily watches, horrified. Are his eyes closed? She cannot tell.

The stripe snakes thin and red across his back. The convict wielding the lash is broad-shouldered. Chosen for his strength.

A wave of nausea rises from her stomach, but still she cannot move.

This time, a stripe, wider, opens the flesh, allowing the blood to flow freely.

At fifty, the doctor steps forward, checks the prisoner, calls, 'Water!' and a leather pail of seawater is thrown over the felon's back.

He writhes, shudders, twisting and clenching his fists above his head. Already, two ribs show white through the flesh, the vertebrae sharp-etched, like hills on a map.

'Continue!' orders the captain of the guard.

'FIFTY-ONE!' The overseer resumes the count.

High above, the wind in the pines builds to a fury.

The doctor takes a step back to keep his shoes from being spattered and stares in dismay at his once-white breeches.

The ground all around them is dark and sodden.

Small bits of flesh lie scattered over the area. Shrubs hold forth tiny morsels, delicate as pink blossoms, suspended momentarily on twigs. Emily is mesmerised. She reaches out as if to touch one, only to turn away in revulsion. Again, she tries to summon the strength to run but cannot.

'ONE HUNDRED!'

She dares not move, knowing she must wait till the end, for fear of being discovered.

The doctor removes his hip flask, takes a quick nip of brandy, to sustain himself.

'ONE HUNDRED AND FIFTY!'

'Enough!' He steps forward and calls a halt to the punishment.

Emily does not need to look to know that the prisoner has slumped unconscious, that only his arms to support him still.

'Release this man,' orders the doctor. 'Put him in solitary.'

'Will he be fit enough to work in the lime kiln tomorrow?' asks the captain of the guard. 'I need men in the salt tower as well.'

'Who knows? He'll not thank you for either,' observes the doctor. 'But I will give my opinion tomorrow, should he last.'

Clouds now shunt their great grey shadows across the shore line, as the man is released and carried by his fellows back to the penitentiary. Emily, suddenly freed from the sight, climbs back down onto the beach and starts to run for the house.

That evening, she dresses plainly in her dark red velvet. She lifts her pearls and is about to place them round her neck when she thinks of the translucent balls of skin she saw today on the bushes and hastily puts the pearls away. James has given them to her but, should he ask, she will say she forgot to wear them.

As they sit at dinner, she sees a frown ruffle his brows as if he is less than pleased with the meal before him and yet it has been months since a ship brought them fresh supplies. Surely he realises she has done her best.

Emily has placed herself between the doctor and the captain of the guard, but though it is her duty to speak of matters that will raise the level of conversation to something more cultured and civilised, tonight she seems more than usually quiet. She listens to the men speak of the brutes in their care. How difficult is the task of keeping them in order. The nature of control, how it should always serve the common good – and does.

She eats listlessly, pushing the food around her plate, showing little appetite.

'Are you all right, my dear?' James appears solicitous in front of his guests.

'Yes, a little tired, that is all.'

'We had a flogging today, Emily. A most depraved wretch. Barely human.' He reaches for the decanter. 'Port, Doctor? Captain?'

'Thank you. Yes,' the doctor says, helping himself and passing it on. 'I doubt he will give you too much trouble now.'

'Good.' The captain replaces the stopper, holds his glass to the candlelight, then says, 'I need more convicts for the lime kiln.'

'You shall have them,' says James.

'They may come with scarred backs,' warns the doctor.

'No matter,' replies the captain.

Emily looks from one to the other. All of these gentlemen treat her with the utmost respect and courtesy. Yet tonight, it is as if she is seeing them for the first time. Strangers.

James reaches across and places a hand over her delicate wrist. He smiles with some concern. 'That is why I would not have you ride out today.'

Love Bytes

Muriel Perkins stares at the trays of meat.

The young butcher, godlike but for acne, emerges from the cool room, shouldering a carcass. He slams it down on the block, whips out a thin-bladed knife and leers at her as he sharpens it. He slices deftly into the ribcage, pops the knife back in its holster and brings down the cleaver, neatly stacking the chops to one side. He tosses a heart on the pile and rummages inside the subcutaneous fat for the kidneys. 'Little beauties, eh?' He juggles them. 'Anything else, love?'

'Mince,' she says, faintly.

He picks up two great handfuls like heavy breasts and dumps them in a bag. 'There you go. Now don't do anything I wouldn't,' he winks.

She floats out, her spirits soaring, only the carry bags weighing her down.

At home, she dumps the bags on the table, goes into her bedroom and changes into operating gear, paper mask and overshoes. She sees herself in the mirror. 'Pity the gloves don't match.'

She sits at her PC and wiggles her fingers. 'Now for the last chapter!'

Be Patient, My Love

Dr Helen Masterman knew what she had to do. All those years of training had prepared her for this moment as she stood at the operating table ready to perform the most difficult, most delicate, most dangerous surgery on the man she loved.

Of course, no one knew. Nothing had been said, no words had passed between them. Theirs was the love of souls, unstated, but for the eyes. Yet she knew Nurse Ashley Fulsome was the only man she could ever love.

When she realised how ill he was, she had almost refused to

operate. 'I can't! My heart is too full to perform a transplant on his.' But she was the only surgeon available. All the others were at a conference, so Ashley's life lay in her hands.

'Scalpel!' She tried to stop the quaver in her voice and still the tremor in her hand. She pared away the flesh and cut through the manly little breast bone, exposing the chop-like rib cage. 'Oh, how sweet!' Then suddenly, before her, lay the red, pulsating heart.

'Throbbing with love.' She sniffed back a tear as she popped in the donor's heart and prepared to sew up her beloved. She rejected blanket and satin stitch in favour of herringbone. Then she stood back and admired the exquisite little stitches, feathered all over his chest.

An hour later, she was holding his hand in Recovery.

'Darling,' he whispered. 'I dreamt I was being caressed and that you took away all my pain.'

'It was nothing, dearest.'

'You know I love you?'

'Oh Ashley, yes!'

'Then as soon as I'm free of all these nasty drips and monitors, we shall be married, my darling.'

The End

Muriel types the title page:

Change of Heart
by
Lavinia Davine

She puts an elastic band round the manuscript, pops it into an envelope and addresses it to her publisher.

'That may be it for a while. I feel a bad case of writer's block, coming on.'

She goes into the kitchen and makes herself a sandwich. She washes up, makes the bed, brings in the washing and waters the potplants.

Next day, she drives to the post office.

'What's this one called, Miss Perkins?' asks the postmistress.

'*Change of Heart*. It's a medical romance.'

'I'll look out for it. I've just read *His Hand On My Heart* and I must say I enjoyed *His Velvet Surprise.*'

'So glad.' Muriel smiles as she feels a popular author should.

The post office is crowded and, as she leaves, a man bumps into her. She observes that he is dark and exotic.

She is opening her car door when she hears a voice behind her.

It is the man from the post office. 'You are beautiful,' he says in a strange, throaty accent.

'Oh?'

It is then that she notices he is exposing himself. Well, at least, a nasty thing like a pork fillet is sticking out of his trousers.

She hears herself saying, 'Well, really!' as she climbs into her car, and checks her make-up in the rear-vision mirror.

Muriel drives home and goes straight to her bedroom. She opens the wardrobe. 'Heiress,' she mutters and takes out two hangers. The pink safari suit with pith helmet and chiffon scarf? Or floaty blue silk with a cartwheel hat? She chooses the silk, adding stockings and high heels.

'My writer's block seems to have gone.'

She sits in front of the PC.

The Jewel is Taken

Sapphire Blade, blue-eyed and beautiful, stepped off the plane and approached the clerk. 'Caa-n't you do somethin' about that haa-tch. Mah luggage'll be ruu-ined.'

'Very sorry.'

'But it's droppin' down so hard, everything'll be broken.' She tossed her masses of blonde hair and stamped her little foot.

Suddenly, someone pressed up close against her and a breathless voice whispered, 'Perhaps I can help?'

She turned to see a man whose long flowing robes could not conceal his bulging biceps. He was rich too, for a jewelled dagger studded with diamonds, rubies and emeralds hung tantalisingly from his waist.

'Say! Are you one of them shee-ikhs?'

'I am from the desert. I have come for you.'

'But what about maah luggage?'

'Leave it, you will not be needing any.' He stared at her opulent breasts and inhaled. His gaze wandered boldly up her long silky legs.

'Well, I don't know. Momma always said never to take candy from strange men.' She sensed he promised her more than candy. 'I just hope I don't come to a sticky end,' she murmured, as she followed him to his limousine. It was unbearably hot, and already she was melting at the knees.

Muriel Perkins sits back. 'Another book! Now to wash the dog and clean out the birdcage.'

Quail

'People change,' he said. 'They don't mean to, they just do.'

She watched as he broke his bread roll into quarters, then eighths. And apportioned butter, meticulously.

The waiter ushered two men past them to a table across the room. He whisked napkins onto their laps and handed them each a menu. With a flourish, he lit the candle.

Left to themselves, the men smiled at each other. One was young, a boy still. Gay, she wondered?

'...and so I think perhaps it would be better if I leave.'

'Pardon?'

'Haven't you been listening?'

She could see he was irritated. 'I was distracted.'

'Obviously. We're supposed to be out. Together,' he said.

'Sorry.'

She bent over her parsnip soup. His was a blood-like borscht. As always, he scooped towards him, as always she dipped away.

'Look, I'm trying to make this as civilised as possible,' he continued.

He was watching her as she added salt. He always said one didn't need it and it irritated him when she added it.

'Yes, I know. Forgive me. You were saying?' she said.

'I think it's better if I leave – if only for a while, until we sort ourselves out.'

'Ourselves?'

'Myself, then.'

'But I thought you had. You said you'd changed.'

'Yes...' he stopped short. 'Don't you want me to stay?' He seemed surprised.

'Not if you'd rather go.'

It hadn't always been this way. Once, just being with each other had been enough. The spark ignited. Now, they barely talked. Words merely extended the daily details of their lives. Soon, there'd be nothing to say.

The waiter appeared and set down their plates. She tried to remember what she'd ordered. Was it beef? Pork? No, the lamb. She looked at his meal. Quail. Two pathetic little mounds on circles of fried bread. Naked, exposed. Vulnerable.

'I don't seem to be able to get through to you any more. You're so...'

'Distant?' she said.

'Yes. Why?'

'I don't know.'

'It's just that sometimes I feel you're trying to shut me out,' he told her.

Slowly the walls had built up around her. Glass. Brick by brick in layered protection. She shouldn't have allowed it to happen, but now that it had, it was the only way she felt safe.

She watched as he plunged his fork into the quail and she turned away.

The men had started with Moët. A celebration? The start of a liaison? Yet the boy was tapping the sides of his chair, fingering the menu, playing with the cutlery. Nervous?

The man probably has a name like – Hugo, she told herself. *And the boy could be – Simon. Hugo*'s smile was just a little tight, as if he were trying too hard to charm the boy. He was of an age where looks were no longer reliable, and charm must prove the catalyst. *Simon may not be ready for that sort of attention*, she thought.

The waiter passed and upended the bottle in its ice bucket, 'Can I get you another bottle, sir?'

'You don't want another one, do you?' He'd decided, it seemed, for both of them.

She opened her mouth to protest, but thought she was probably better off without it.

She remembered a couple she'd seen once, on a train. They'd sat from Central to Kempsey not saying a word, just staring ahead. At Kempsey, he'd gone to the buffet car and come back with two pies. He handed her one and they'd eaten them in silence.

She looked across and saw the man raising his glass in a toast. What could he be saying? *Hugo* appeared to do all the talking, or was it entertaining? *Simon* was merely listening. *Is he happy?* she wondered.

The man no doubt had money and influence. Wit, sophistication, almost everything, it seemed.

She realised he was talking and she heard herself saying, 'If you're not happy, there's no point in your staying.'

Why was he persisting? Didn't he want to go? Why extend the pain?

She wondered if he felt the gap between them as pain. Immutable, tangible – a heavy ache behind the eyes with unshed tears. She could sense he was hurting, but the wall between them was such that she could no longer reach him.

They went on eating in silence. She looked back at the men…

Hugo could buy *Simon* clothes and textbooks – whatever a student, and she felt he must be a student, needed. Rent boys they called them. Though he didn't look like rent. He seemed rather a novice. He lacked the confidence of one who knows how to market his body. The thin hands and long fingers suggested a musician, but the shoulders implied he worked out a bit. Confronted as he was by an offer of patronage, she could see all he really wanted was love.

Perhaps if there'd been children, they might have bonded to each other. Or been bound? Prisoners to past acts based on feelings long since dead. She looked at the boy and thought of him as a son, her son. Motherless, from across the room, she ached to hold him to show that she cared.

'It seems to me that neither of us,' he was choosing his words, 'are getting much out of the relationship.' And to cover himself, he added, 'Don't you agree?'

She nodded absently, then said. 'I don't think I've been what you wanted. I know I irritate you and I should have been more malleable. Something you could have moulded into a corporate wife.'

'Nonsense,' he said, but she could see he agreed.

She noticed that *Hugo* had claimed the boy's hand on the table as his eyes searched the boy's face.

Simon seemed suddenly embarrassed, as if to remove his hand would prove a slight, yet to leave it prisoner implied surrender. She watched the pain of confusion on his face but when he suddenly looked across and saw her, she turned her head away.

She had the feeling that the man was winning. She felt angry, protective. She wanted to warn the boy. *Hugo* had made some witticism and *Simon* had laughed, despite himself. The tension started to flow away. Maybe the boy didn't wish to be claimed but had no way of declining, as if his hand were somehow separate from his feelings.

A young girl came into the restaurant with a basket of roses.

He turned to look at her but, as she approached, gestured her away. 'They're parasites, you know,' he said. 'The way they come up to you. They hang around and even though they see you're not interested they still zoom in for a possible sale.'

'They don't make much. Barely a living,' she said. 'They get more knock-backs than sales.'

'Life has its knock-backs.'

She felt sure this wasn't him talking, that his inner turmoil was surfacing as cold facts.

From across the room, she saw the older man hail the flower-seller. His smile was almost possessive as he presented the rose.

The young man blushed.

That could have been my rose, she thought. There was a time when he'd bought her roses. Spontaneously. A declaration of sorts. Now it seemed there was nothing to declare. Merely matters to sort.

Once, she'd been like the young man, passive. She was watching him go down the same path. If he allowed it, he would easily slip into dependence, without control.

The older man craved someone to admire him. His charm was little comfort by itself. In return, he could be generous at a time when the boy needed it. *Hugo* saw himself as a guardian, no doubt. What sort of guardian, was a matter for conjecture.

'...I thought nearby, so we can still see each other if we need to.'

Need to or want to? she wondered. Perhaps he had a flat in mind?

'You don't need my approval,' she said. 'If you've seen a flat you like...'

'I didn't say I'd found one.'

'No.' She placed her knife and fork together. Carefully, thinking, *Perhaps we've finished with more than the meal.*

'Dessert?' he asked.

'Just coffee.'

Across the room, she saw *Simon* had withdrawn his hand but *Hugo's* still rested on the table. To show he claimed more than the space, perhaps. Maybe he realises the price extracted for generosity, he wants arm's length to decide, space to manoeuvre. An escape even, if one presents itself. *He probably suspects he's gay but is unsure of his feelings. Hugo's old enough to be his father,* she thought.

He'd signalled the waiter. 'Two cappuccinos, please.'

'I'd prefer flat white, thank you,' she told the waiter.

The victory was small, but precious.

'Do you think they love each other?' she thought aloud.

'Who?'

'The men. Over there. Or is it just sex and a free meal?'

'Must you be crude?'

'What do you suppose he does? The older one?' she asked.

'How should I know? Does it matter?'

'I suppose not. But he'd only know the company of people his own age. That man sees him as an investment. Dinners, theatre, clothes. Dressing a mannikin to undress later.'

'Your mind does jump about. It's really none of your business what he's doing. Besides, I thought we were discussing us.'

'All right, when do you move?'

Hugo, she saw, had also ordered quail. As it was set in front of him, she was aware that the boy was looking at her. *Are they talking about us,*

I wonder? Do we have that look of intimate disinterest, the combination of rust and resentment?

Hugo was trying to maintain the boy's attention. He stretched out and lifted a brown tendril of hair away from the eyes and spoke. The boy laughed.

They looked down at their plates and as *Hugo* pinned the quail down for consumption, she saw the boy shudder. Did he see himself on the plate? *Hugo* had caught him at a point in life when he could go either way. *Hugo* would make sure it was his. The boy was considering options and playing for time.

'...then tomorrow I'll make arrangements. I'm glad we'll still be friends,' he was saying. 'I'll take some of my things with me and collect the rest later.'

'What about books, pictures?'

'You decide. All I need now is furniture and linen.' He reached across and touched her hand. 'I'm sure it's for the best.'

Hugo dabbed at the corners of his mouth and called for dessert.

The boy shook his head as the waiter took his plate.

Hugo's appetite seemed voracious. Would *Simon* be next? She thought of him as her *Simon* now.

She could see he was trapped, consumed in an endless debt of gratitude from which there was no escape. She was conscious that he was looking at her again.

Her husband saw it too. 'Do you know that boy? You've been staring at him all evening.'

'Not really, he just reminds me of...' she trailed off.

He dealt with the bill, she put on her jacket. She wanted to say something to the boy but could think of nothing. Relationships started, while others ended.

The waiter placed a dish of profiteroles in front of *Hugo*, whose face glowed.

As she stood up, she turned for one last look at *Simon*. He smiled faintly at her and she thought she saw him shrug.

Mr Brown Goes Out

It was a fella at work gave Joe the name and an address in Kings Cross. 'Ask for Mick.' Joe planned on something for their anniversary. He wasn't good with dates. Never had been. He often forgot her birthday so Thelma had to remind him, but this being their tenth wedding anniversary, she'd been dropping hints for days.

He'd exchanged his overalls for his one and only suit and was on a tram heading up to the Cross. Not that he wasn't wary of anything black market. He'd had his fingers burnt once before when a bottle of sly grog turned out more metho than gin and by then the bloke had scarpered with his dough. But Joe sensed this Mick character was on the level, so it was worth a try and what with a war, there wasn't much choice on his wages. He was after a bottle of gin and maybe some sweet sherry, Thelma's favourite.

Most of his friends were in the army fighting overseas, but he'd been knocked back. Poor eyesight, they told him, even though he said he was fine with glasses and they said, 'Yeah, but you got to be able to see to shoot straight. Besides, what if they break?' At school, he'd been called Bottles, for bottle glasses.

He knew others who'd been knocked back. One mate lost his leg as a sixteen-year-old, running for a tram in Pitt Street. A car came up behind him and took it clean off below the knee. He'd had a wooden leg ever since. Like a skinny wine barrel strapped to the stump. But it hadn't stopped him fronting up, boasting he could march and swim with the best of them. Ride a bike too if he had to, but the sergeant shook his head and said, 'And who'll piggyback you out the jungle if you slip and break it?'

Now they both worked in the same place, making aeroplane parts. Before the war, the factory made fridges, then the machines were converted and now you couldn't buy a fridge if you tried.

Okay, so it wasn't like the Blitz in London, but they still had air-raid sirens and Sydney had its own brown-out with all neon signs off, only soft pools of light falling from street lights and otherwise everything else dark, supposed to keep the city safe from the Japs – if they landed. And no street signs for ten miles inland to make it harder. That's assuming the buggers could read English. Buildings all had their blinds and blackout paper and houses, heavy curtains. Black caps covered car lights and instrument panels were dimmed.

All this half light gave the Cross an eerie feel, like some huge stage set or scene from a movie where everything was both strange and familiar. Like people were up to no good somehow. They went about their business still, hurrying wherever it was they were headed, and if you saw a couple busy in a doorway, you might wonder but turned away out of politeness, and maybe next day there'd be a used condom on the ground as evidence. People lived for the moment and who could blame them? Here today, gone tomorrow, was the byword. Maybe for good.

Tram destination panels were blinkered either side so you could only read them if you stood in front, hoping to hell the driver saw you before he ran you down. Inside the carriage was dim too and he asked the trammy how she managed to give the right change every time. 'Took a bit of getting used to,' she said, 'pennies and florins being the same size, but florins is heavier.'

Trams could cause chaos too. The government had to make do, patching and re-patching with whatever parts they could get, but things went wrong. There was the time the brakes on a Broadway tram failed and it screeched downhill, crashing into a stationary tram near Mountain Street, and sixty people killed. The injured ended up in Prince Alfred Casualty.

The tram had reached Kings Cross now and he got off at the Hotel to make his way down Victoria Street looking for 145. It turned out to be a terrace like those either side but less grand. More 'lived in'. Rundown. He pressed the button but there was no answer at first then a voice said, 'Yes?'

'My name's Joe Brown. I'm looking for Mick.'

'Mick? What do you want him for?'

'I'm told he could have a package for me,' remembering what he'd been told to say.

'Upper floor, No. 8, room at the back.'

Years of cooked onions and old cabbage assailed his nostrils as he groped his way up the dark staircase. A single globe hanging from the ceiling was all between him and tripping.

Mick stood in the doorway of a room with bed, armchair and table, triangular basin squeezed into one corner and an old dresser, paint peeling in layers of white and green.

'What package?'

'I was thinking gin, and a bottle of sweet sherry maybe?'

'I can't promise anything. It'll be whatever I get. And it'll cost you.'

'I don't mind. Within reason. See what you can do. It's for the missus. Our tenth anniversary.'

'I don't have anything here. Come back in an hour. And you can't wait here.'

'But it's gone six. The pubs'll be closed. What'll I do?'

'Get yourself a coffee at the Hasty Tasty. Up the top of the road.'

The door shut behind him and he made his way downstairs, hand firm on the bannisters. Since it was Friday, the streets were already busy with more people about. Men in uniform. Some women too. Others flashily dressed, ready to party. Kings Cross was no theatre of war but it carried its own sense of danger. Most of the toffs had fled their fancy apartments for the Blue Mountains, leaving those who'd moved in at bargain rates ready to party.

He bought a *Mirror* from the paper boy on the corner and crossed the road to the Hasty Tasty. Slipping into an empty booth, he reminded himself the coffee would be essence, chicory-based, tasting nothing like the coffee he knew.

'What'll it be?' The waitress sounded tired already as if at the end of her shift not the start.

'Coffee. White. No sugar. The wife made me give it up. To save coupons.'

'Good for her. Be back in a jiff.'

He opened the paper for the hour's wait, but since no one was eyeing his table, he relaxed. He read the news, scanned the sporting pages, then borrowed a pencil from the waitress for the crossword.

When the hour was up, he paid and left, returning the pencil with a wink and a 'Thanks, love,' keen to see what Mick had got for him.

He beamed. 'Gin and sherry! I can't wait for Thelma's face.'

'You owe me twelve quid.'

'Twelve pounds!'

'Take it or leave it. There's plenty of others keen enough.'

'No. It's all right. Just more than I was expecting.'

He held the brown paper bag close to his chest as he headed for the tram. *You've done yourself proud, Joe Brown. It'll leave you short for the week but it'll be worth it.*

It was suddenly much cooler. A sharp wind had set in and he pulled up the collar of his austerity suit against it.

Later, inside the Hasty Tasty, a constable was interviewing the waitress. She'd been crying and the manager had told her to take the rest of the night off.

'I'd gone out for a cigarette. A five-minute break since we weren't busy. That's when I saw him. He'd been in for a coffee earlier and I was thinking, *Nice man. Gentlemanly. Not like some round here.* Then he suddenly stepped off the kerb and the car hit him. He had this dark suit on, and the driver probably didn't see him. It all happened so fast but the funny thing was, as he fell, he looked like he was trying to save what was in the paper bag.'

Thelma placed the plate on the saucepan. I'm off to bed. I thought this time, maybe. But he's forgotten again and I'll bet he's been at the pub and now he's shickered. But he won't have forgotten his tea.

The People on the Bus Go Up and Down

Joyce tapped her Opal card and found a seat. *At least boarding at the start gets me a window.*

A young woman was struggling aboard, asking the driver to wait while she juggled a chunky pink stroller under the sign saying, Please Give Up This Seat For The Elderly, before going back to haul up a larger, black suitcase which she parked in the aisle.

Joyce seated diagonally opposite, glared disapproval. *She's not leaving that in the aisle? I'll be saying something if she does.*

The woman bent over the child, tucking a blanket over its legs, talking softly.

African kiddy? Adopted clearly. And she's put bows in its hair to match the stroller. How quaint.

As the woman sank wearily into the seat, Joyce had the strange feeling she'd seen her before. *I can't remember where. Either that or she has one of those faces you recognise. Like those tests of different faces, different races, and you have to guess where they're from. Bother! Now I'll sit here all trip wondering where I've seen her.*

It reminded her of that time, years ago, when her mother was doing a crossword. 'Who wrote *East Lynne*?' she asked and Joyce couldn't think. Then next morning at breakfast her mother blurted out, 'Mrs Henry Wood.'

'Pardon?'

'Mrs Henry Wood wrote *East Lynne*. I've been lying awake half the night trying to remember. You know, "Dead! Dead! and never called me mother".'

Joyce chuckled at the memory.

The bus was well underway and again she turned to the young

woman. *Maybe it was in a magazine? At the hairdresser's, perhaps? Or the doctor's?* These were the only places she read magazines. *All that stupid gossip about celebrities I've never heard of. But she's not one of them. If she were, she wouldn't be in a bus, but a stretch limo. Especially with a kiddy and that big suitcase. Maybe she's an actress, in one of the soaps?*

It was while she was staring, that the woman suddenly turned and stared back, riveting Joyce like a pinned and venomous spider. Joyce pretended she'd actually been looking out the window, but the woman remained unconvinced.

Then Joyce noticed the stroller. Only – it wasn't, it was a small wheelchair, festooned with rattles and fluffy animals, making the dark-skinned, toddler with her peppercorn curls seem positively exotic.

And disabled.

I wish I'd never caught the bus. I nearly didn't. I was thinking of getting a taxi, since it looked like rain, but the walk home from the bus would do me good. Besides, I need to watch my pennies.

She hadn't really noticed the child, so busy was she trying to re-member the mother's face, but the young woman clearly thought oth-erwise. Joyce regretted she wasn't close enough to apologise, explain that she looked *familiar.* But it would only sound fake.

Then she remembered where. There'd been this TV documentary on adoption, how far fewer children were available. So now disabled kids and those from Third World countries were being given a chance. The woman was interviewed as an adopting parent. *I remember thinking 'How kind'. You could only admire someone prepared to devote her life to caring for a child who wasn't hers and who wouldn't have stood a chance.*

Joyce was trying desperately to think how to make amends. She'd hurt a complete stranger. Inadvertently perhaps, but nonetheless un-forgiveable. She could almost hear her mother appalled, saying, 'Joyce, how could you! It's so rude to stare.'

At that moment, the young woman, having revived a little, stood up and began manoeuvring the heavy suitcase up the aisle to the luggage rack, where, with an almighty heave, she hoisted it over the bars.

Oh dear, I would have helped. If you'd said. Again Joyce realised her missed opportunity. The young woman resumed her seat casting a There, happy now? glare at Joyce.

Never mind, if she gets off before me, I'll offer to help then. And if not, when my stop comes, I'll make sure to apologise. That way, at least, she'll know I'm not completely lacking in feeling.

The young woman reached across and lifted the child out of the wheelchair. The little one's head lolled on her chest and her eyes showed no recognition of the woman or her surroundings. The mother settled the child, cradling her arms about her, bending her head, whispering murmurs of love.

Joyce felt at once privileged to witness such intimacy, their heads so close, but at the same time embarrassed, as if she were some sort of voyeur, especially since the young woman was protecting the child from the likes of Joyce. The sticky-beaks, hard-hearted, indifferent, unchari- table, and yes, she had to admit, cruel people she had come to represent. Now she was even more determined to bend down and say how sorry she was, that she'd seen the program on TV and thought she was simply wonderful.

At the next stop, a giggle of students boarded, after that, office work- ers, nine-to-fivers. Businessmen and women rushing home for evening meals now packed the aisle and Joyce could no longer see the woman or her child. She would have to fight her way through when her stop came to reach them, but fight she would.

She pressed the stop button early, readied her stick and shopping bag, then, excusing herself, pushed past the man beside her as he swung his knees into the aisle to let her pass. The doors slid back and more people surged on board leaving Joyce to push her way through to tap her Opal. *Oh please. Wait! What if the doors close and I get carried on an- other two blocks and have to walk all the way back?*

At last she made it out and found herself on the pavement staring as the bus drove off, seeing the head of a young woman bent over her child and imagined her softly singing, cradling the child in loving arms.

A Handcart in the Street

It is the will of Allah, Lord of the Worlds, that I, Halil, lie here. Who knows why one man does not stand like another and his legs are thin and wasted within his clothes? Allah, perhaps?

My brother, Serif, dresses me. He carries me down to the handcart and pushes me each day to a street far from the rattle of traffic. Today there is no wind to stir the dust in the streets and I rest near a corner, the better to claim those who pass on their way to prayer.

Bayram had begun. Four days of sacrifice. Already some buy pieces of lamb for their feast on the last night and sheep and goats are tethered for killing on waste land. Serif tells me those in the flat above us borrowed a car to bring two sheep from the country. But when the car stopped, the sheep would not jump from the boot. So the one they dragged out by the horns as they pulled at the fleece of the other.

Families with trucks will share a cow. Our friends cut up their cow at the end of the street and the blood ran down over the cobbles and into the gutter.

You cat – off with you! I have nothing to give you. Go to the alleys where they cut up meat and beg there.

That man on the corner, the one in fine clothes. It is a magnificent bird that sits on his wrist. A falcon requires a cord to secure it, a leather hood to keep its eyes from sighting prey. My prey is always before me, yet I need no cord to tie me here. You give me a coin. Should I be grateful? A pittance? What will that buy me?

Serif earns wages. My sister is married, why therefore should I burden the old age of my parents? Propped on my side, I stretch out my palm, imploring. And when the arm aches, do I rest it? Some days, Allah is willing and the people give. Not so much that I can be tithed, but a little.

Today when the Grand Bazaar is closed, there will be few selling their wares. Still, some on the streets may be disposed to offer alms. For Allah, the Beneficent, the Merciful.

Almost by itself, my head turns at the sound of voices. Will you? Ah! blessings be upon you. My fingers close over the tiny note before it flutters away on the greedy wind.

Women do not notice me. Passing in black behind their husbands, their daughters obedient in dark blue. Who knows if their eyes move behind their veils? But I importune no man's wife.

My sister brings me a glass of tea to refresh me when it is hot. Sometimes the yoghurt or halva seller will stop nearby and I might claim a morsel or the scrapings of a bowl.

Today I am fasting. Only when the boy with his tray of sesame seed rings sets up his stool beside me does my stomach remind me that I have not eaten. Go, leave me. Sell elsewhere. Why must I smell your wares? Ah, cigarette. Thank you, sir. The smoke spirals towards my nostrils. Enough to break the sameness of this and every day. Maybe you will pass this way again? Tomorrow perhaps? That is a fine fish the old fellow carries. Lamb, goat are luxuries when fish may be caught from the bridge. And those they cannot eat they sell. Did you catch that yourself? Hold it firmly for the tail is slippery and take care not to drop it. Other eyes watch from the doorways. The cats are thin and hungry, they avoid the boots of the crowd but when the crowd has gone, they come from the shadows and will eat anything.

Perhaps I should sell something, if not to my countrymen, to the foreigners who are foolish with their money. Dishes of birdseed for them to feed the pigeons? Postcards, views? I could lie outside the mosque and watch them take off their shoes to enter. A walnut? And from your own pocket too. Salaam, it is a gesture of friendship, and I thank you.

Serif carries me to the mosque sometimes, placing me on the mats. The dark peace is soothing, and I lie there forgetting what life is like outside. He says he will take me to see the relics of the Prophet, His Holy Footprint, His Letter, His Tooth and the Hair from His Beard.

Serif has spoken of them, and it would please me to see them, yet I fear I may be overcome when I do.

There goes Tarik, the albino, to the market stalls. His small brother Yusef leads him by the hand for the sun is fierce on his pale eyes and he squints to avoid it. Together they load the tables in the street with shoes and clothes and for that the merchants will pay them a little. There – they saw me greet them.

Go. Move away from my place. This is my ground for begging. What right have you to set up your lottery beside me? Everyone knows the rabbit is trained. It chooses only the marbles smeared with food. And when the foreigners have gone with the summer, you will eat the rabbit and train another. Where too do the bears and camels go in winter, when no one wishes to take their photographs? Do the bears still pose or dance when there is no one to watch them? Perhaps they take off their muzzles and harness ribbons and run free? Would that I... But I must not presume to question the will of Allah.

Already the nights are cold and longer, the wood and straw is piled high on the balconies for the coming months.

Someone has emptied a pail from their doorway. Water trickles down the pavement and collects in pools where the marble is broken. Now my handcart sits in water. I am surrounded by it and Serif will wet his shoes when he comes to take me home.

You soldier – alms? For the love of Allah? And how am I to know what the army pays you? Your bayonet is old, but your wages new. Your friend there, the machine gun, is he disposed to pity a beggar? Apologies, apologies, you have more pressing matters it seems. If walking the streets with a swagger and close-cropped hair is pressing. Enough, enough, I'll hold my tongue. You did not choose the army, the army chose you.

It is cooler now. A wind springs up and stirs the dirt and papers and the faithful are called to prayer. A lone dog elsewhere in the city answers the call. In the streets, merchants pack up their goods and cover their stalls. The foreigners have returned to their hotels in taxis, for their feet are tired. They will sit with drinks in their hands watching the sun crown with gold the dark waters of the Bosporus. For me it is enough to know that it sets, and that Serif is coming for me.

Ah! he comes now. Mind you remove the stone that holds the hand-cart on the pavement, lest someone trip on it. Let us go. As we travel, you will tell me of your day, and I will recall mine. No great riches, a little, enough. When one cannot work for one's bread, one must accept. And who am I to question the will of Allah, the Beneficent, the Merci-ful? It is enough that I am living.

One Plain, One Purl, Two Sugars

When Edna felt ready, she knitted herself a teapot.

A nice brown woollen affair, with bobbles sticking to the sides and lid, to the handle and spout, so the brown tea inside will forever bubble with steam.

She'd knitted as a child, using up scraps of wool, listening to the clack-clicking of needles as her grandmother and aunts dropped little stitches of wisdom her way.

'Two women and a goose make a market.'

'Choose neither women nor linen by candlelight.'

'Wash your face in the dew of the first of May and you will have a fine complexion and find a husband.'

Not that it's done them much good, they're spinsters, even if they do have fine complexions.

Her mother sewed. For a living, since Edna's father was killed in the war. Blown to pieces, her grandmother used to say.

Edna preferred to remember him in uniform, as he looked the day he left, his photograph on the mantelepiece just above her head, till she grew big enough to look him in the face.

Her mother sewed baby dresses, row upon row of tiny stitches, creating frills and flounces, puffed sleeves, exquisite lace edging, sometimes even smocking.

Only once did her mother make something larger – a dress for Edna, on the toy sewing machine she was getting for her birthday. The needle pierced a row of neat little holes in the yellow organza, the S-wheel beneath, looping back and forth, snatching the thread to form stitches as small and neat as the rows her mother sewed by hand.

Edna learnt to sew on that machine, although she still preferred knitting. As she grew older, other things claimed her attention, and she put her knitting aside, always knowing some day she'd come back to it.

There were knitters everywhere in those days, women on trains and buses, knitting away time till they reached their stop; in the half-light of cinemas, staring at the screen, the clickety-clack of needles pausing only to change rows, tug at the wool in their bags, or sometimes in the sad bits, to rummage for a hanky.

The years Edna was too busy to knit seemed to sum up the rest of her life. From the time she left school to become a secretary because she couldn't think of anything else to do, till years later and the day Reg told her he was leaving because he needed his own space. Then he added, 'I'll be back later for my tools.'

Good. The nasty things leave sawdust all over the shed floor. Not to mention the great hulking sit-on lawnmower he never uses.

Not that Reg's 'finding himself' had anything to do with the office bimbo currently filling his space, or more to the point, he hers, but when the front door slammed behind him, Edna suddenly realised she'd never done anything without Reg. Whatever he'd insisted they do, they did.

Perhaps it was living in each other's pockets, but I thought it was the way he liked it. Anyway, he's probably fonder of his tools than he is of me. His circular saw, for instance, the angle grinder and carry case, his random orbit sander, the thirteen-millimetre impact drill, his router and multi-saw not to mention his hammer drill. Reg is a sucker for tools and catalogues. He haunts hardware stores and the shed's full of his noisy toys.

Not that his mania stopped at the tool shed. He was mad about household appliances too and had bought her every electrical gadget a woman could possible want. And more.

I can chop, mince, slice, pare, grate, shred, julienne, pulverise or purée whatever's on the bench. Then I can boil it, broil it, roast, bake, steam, stew, or sauté it, and while it's cooking, fluff up some rice, whip up a waffle, or juggle jaffles like an expert.

If after all that she felt worn out and her brain was sludging around like an ice cream churn, at the flick of a switch she could grind her own coffee beans and make a simulated cappuccino.

I can reduce a carrot to its molecular structure, but whatever happened to the rest of my life?

Reg seemed to think she derived as much pleasure from kitchen gadgets as he did from power tools.

Mind you, his first attempt at putting up shelves was a disaster and from then on I never asked what he was actually making in the shed. The sound of whirring and hammering, drilling and sanding went on all the time, but there never anything to show for it. He probably went in there just to get away from me, and since noise meant power tools to Reg he just turned on all his gadgets at once. As long as they were shrilling and buzzing, grinding and drilling, he was at peace with the world. A sort of mechanical Om that brought him to a state of Nirvana. Well, frankly, I need more than the whine of a food processor to give me a buzz.

Of course, she always thanked him politely for each new appliance. After all, he meant well and they were labour-saving.

If I don't count the time spent washing every one of the multiple parts. But I was happy to go along with it, till he brought home the knitting machine.

He dumped it on the coffee table and said, 'Here, now you can knit me a jumper.'

'I don't need a machine to knit!' she told him.

'But I've never seen you knitting. Anyway, I'm going to be spending a bit of time interstate. I thought this way you wouldn't be lonely.'

'And I don't need a machine for company!'

So the De Luxe Digital Knitting Mate sat unopened in its box and Reg went interstate.

After one such trip, he walked out for good and Edna remembered one of her grandmother's pearls of advice, 'Let the sufferer from toothache fill his mouth with cold spring water and sit beside the fireplace till the water boils.'

Reg is my toothache, a nagging throb in my jaw. Not only that, he's deceived me and that's unacceptable.

'In water you see your face, in wine the heart of another,' her grandmother had warned her.

Now I come to think of it, there were signs, stray whiffs of perfume, cheap and nasty, and dinners missed, when his plate sat on a saucepan of boiling water, till he wandered in saying, 'I've eaten,' then I'd give it to the cat.

'Buttons, things are going to change around here. You're going on a diet.'

Buttons hissed and heaved himself onto the kitchen cupboards while Edna rang for a locksmith.

Then she climbed to the attic to retrieve her old sewing machine. Taking Reg's jumpers, she cut them up into big bold squares and triangles, diamonds and oblongs, trapezes and rhomboids, and sewed them all together in a luscious rebellion of colour, finishing up with a throwover for the coffee table.

When Reg came back and found the locks changed, he was furious. He banged and thumped on the doors to no avail; Edna had gone shopping. He thought of breaking in – after all, he had tools for it, but was it breaking and entering if it was still his house? In the end, he just left a note saying, 'You'll be sorry. Who'll protect you?' Forgetting of course, that since he'd left anyway, the question was hypothetical.

The shed was not locked, so he packed the car with his tools, leaving only the sit-on lawnmower, which he wouldn't be needing in his new apartment. He did take the De Luxe Digital Knitting Mate, however, because he didn't have any jumpers and his live-in secretary might be prepared to make some for him. If he asked nicely.

Soon after, Edna arrived home with a large box of wool and a supply of needles and began to knit.

At first, she dropped stitches and lost her place in the pattern, and the wool dropped off her knee and rolled under the couch, where Buttons wrestled it into submission.

'Practice is all I need,' she said, rescuing the wool. And within a day or so she was creating scarves and mittens, caps and vests, beanies and mufflers, as if she'd never stopped. So proficient was she, she decided to tackle something more challenging. 'A teapot! I'm tired of that electric tea maker, I'd like a good old-fashioned pot, brown, so the stains don't show. Grandmother always said our insides must be quite discoloured with tea.'

She knitted it in brown, making sure the handle was heat-resistant and adding a good curved spout to avoid drips. As she knitted, she added chunky bobbles on the sides, 'Like the knobbly bits you sometimes see on china ones.'

Then she thought she'd knit a few cups and saucers, and teaspoons to go with them, and a good round tray. She filled the cups with brown woollen tea, a strong colour, though not as dark as her teapot, and made a sugar bowl with gleaming white sugar. For this, she chose a rather sparkly wool.

All this made her hungry and she began to think about afternoon tea. So she knitted up a nice cake plate in a lovely blue with a butterfly on it and a solid cake stand, in a smart red. While she was doing that, she thought about the cakes her grandmother used to make and that maybe she should knit up a batch. So she chose a range of pastels and knitted some dear little cupcakes with pretty icing, adding chopped-up coloured wool, like sprinkles, on top.

The big cake proved more of a problem. She considered a tipsy cake but wasn't sure which colour to use for the sherry. Then she thought a Dundee might be nice, but the white wool she'd need for almonds looked dull against the brown. And she didn't fancy a simnel cake.

All that creamy wool marzipan might be too heavy and rich.

Finally, she opted for a good old-fashioned fruit cake.

Not a boiled one, mind, where the colour of the fruit isn't bright and glossy, but Grandmother's pound cake. A pound of butter to a pound of sugar – and the rest as follows.

She chose a rich glossy tan for the brown sugar, a lovely pale gold for the butter and away she went, knitting at a fast pace to keep it all light and airy. She folded the gleaming colours of fruit into the spicy white wool she'd chosen for the flour and, when she considered the cake done and cooled, she set it carefully on the stand. Next she knitted a smart navy wrapper to go round it. On top she put a thick layer of royal icing (using moss stitch to keep the texture thick and even) and spread it with a few woollen fruits she'd kept aside specially.

After all, what sort of rich dark fruit cake would it be without royal icing and glacé fruit?

After a week of solid knitting, she took herself off for a break, on a bus tour. And it just so happened that the woman next to her turned out to be a knitter too, so they swapped patterns.

'All those lovely colours and textures, and the wool, warm and soft, trickling through your fingers,' said Edna.

'I like the sound the needles make.' The woman lowered her voice and whispered, 'I find all that clickiting quite – well, stimulating.'

Edna arrived home full of ideas inspired by the people she'd seen on the bus. She'd noted their features, their colouring, birthmarks, defects, habits, quirks, funny gaits, even their hands and fingernails.

Anything's possible in wool if you only set your mind to it.

Next day, she went out and bought more wool, more needles, and started knitting again. Buttons yawned and climbed onto her lap. He settled into a ball as pale and sandy as the wool she was using, flicking his tail as he lulled himself into the gentle rhythm of sleep. Edna knitted on. And on.

When she got up, two days later, she had knitted herself three new friends, each one a knitter.

There was Marge, who wore her hair short and permed and who'd had an operation for cataracts. Her eyes looked large and startled behind her green glasses. But she could see well enough and was just starting a pink jumper for her granddaughter who was turning three.

Lovely kiddy, she told Edna.

Marge felt the cold badly and went in for knitted stockings in bright colours, and long bloomers, although the elastic had a habit of giving up so the legs sometimes dangled a bit below her skirt.

Then there was Jean. She wore a hairnet because, truth to tell, she was a bit bald and wore a wig. But since she couldn't afford a good one, she'd had to settle for one a little too big.

The hairnet helps keep it in place, she told Edna.

She'd knitted one with sparkles, so she'd look presentable when she went to the TAB. She was busy knitting a shopping bag with an All-Bran label on the side, to remind her that she was fresh out.

Then there was Mavis. She was a bit of a worrier. About chills mostly. So she'd knitted herself a beanie to keep her head warm. She was a great one for using up scraps of wool in all sorts of ways, like rugs and waistcoats.

And I always use a sewing machine for the seams. It makes them that much stronger than sewing by hand, she told Edna.

She hated to see woollens thrown out. As soon as they showed any sign of wear, she unravelled them and made something new from the good bits. She'd just started undoing the leg of her slacks and was using it to knit an all-in-one jump suit for a baby, in bright orange.

Young mothers nowadays go in for these bright colours and it will keep some little mite toasty warm.

Edna went off to bed quite worn-out. She'd knitted Marge and Jean and Mavis with open mouths, and they'd made full use of them. Still, she couldn't complain, she was glad of the company, and it was certainly more than Reg had offered, down there in his tool shed or busy with his corporate affairs. As soon as she hit the pillow she fell sound asleep, while Buttons snuggled into the small of her back and purred.

Down near the fence, he saw her light go out. He waited a while then, forcing the lock on the kitchen window, climbed inside. Bruce was your typical burglar – old woollen jumper that had shrunk, knitted balaclava, one size too small, but that didn't stop him searching the drawers for money and rummaging through the sideboard.

He was tiptoeing upstairs when he caught sight of Marge, Jean and Mavis, still with their mouths open.

One plain, one purl, two sugars and just a dash of milk. Good and strong. That's fine, thanks.

The hairs on the back of his neck rose, tingling. His head began pounding from the loud CLACK-CLICKING of needles and, his not to reason why, Bruce turned and fled.

But as he climbed back through the kitchen window, he caught himself on a nail and tore off a little piece of his elbow. Not stopping to retrieve it, he fled down the garden and leapt over the fence.

It's just not fair. A bloke can't earn a decent living any more. He'd be forced to go straight.

Inside, Marge was wondering, What say we knit that nice young man a jumper? He certainly needs one.

Yes, and perhaps a balaclava? suggested Jean. I'm good on them.

And I'm sure he's not really bad. Just a bit down on his luck.

So each of them knitted a stitch in time to save Bruce.

Next morning, Edna woke up feeling quite refreshed. She padded downstairs in her knitted moccasins to find Marge, Jean and Mavis, hard at it.

'Morning, girls,' she said opening the front door. She picked up the newspaper and draped it over her arm. Then she saw the note on the mat.

She peered to decipher the untidy stitches.

LORNS MOWD CHEEP. RING BRUCE.

'Oh yes, they do look bad, I've been too busy to notice and there's that perfectly good sit-on lawnmower just lying idle. Well, I'll give Bruce a ring after breakfast.

Behind their knitting, the trio beamed.

Edna went into the kitchen and was just filling the red woollen kettle at the sink, when she spotted the little tanned patch of wool clinging to the nail.

That's odd. It looks like part of someone's elbow. Oh well, I'll put it somewhere safe till I find out who it belongs to.

'Now, who wants a cuppa?' she called.

Love one, came the reply.

What the Sea Rejects

Lenny Duff, aged fourteen, 1931: We were down the beach that morning, me and my mate Jimmy. We usually go down early of a Saturday looking for stuff. Shells and pebbles, bits of driftwood, anything really that Mum can make into things to sell at the markets. Ornaments like. It's 1931, but money's still tight even with Dad working down the Moruya quarry. That's where they ship the big blocks of granite up to Sydney for the Harbour Bridge. Mum says it's dangerous work and a couple of men got killed there a while back, but it's dangerous on the bridge too. Fall off and you're dead by the time you hit the water.

Sometimes I find a penny, or tanner, she lets me keep and me and Jimmy hang round till the fisherman come in to clean their nets, hoping they'll maybe give us a fish. But that morning Jimmy's up the beach waving his arms, yelling, 'Hey! Get a squiz at this!' and I can see this bundle of wet clothes.

So I race up, thinking he's found something interesting. But turns out it's a woman and kid, drowned. We've never seen anyone dead before, so we're a bit shaky like, 'specially as the kid's only little, younger than us. There's sand on his feet and his mum's hair's all matted with bits of seaweed. At first, we don't know what to do, we're too scared to move almost, but we know we got to tell someone and I says for him to stay there while I head off up the beach to find a cottage to have them ring the cops.

Then when I get back he says, 'The kid's dead. I'm not sure about his mum, but. You think we should we roll 'em over and see?'

'No, don't touch 'em,' I says. 'We got to wait till the coppers get here,' and that takes another ten minutes.

Then an ambulance comes and the ambo kneels down and has a

real good look and asks the constable for a knife to cut the belt tied round them.

And next thing, there's cops everywhere telling us to stand back and not leave the beach and asking questions, like what we're doing there, and they make me open my bag to show I haven't nicked nothing and they load them onto stretchers, throw a grey blanket over the kid's face and the ambulance drives off.

After that, we don't feel like waiting for the fishermen, and clear off home.

On the way, Jimmy says, 'How'd you think they got there?', because the beach is only good for scrounging. You wouldn't want to swim there on account of the storm water drain and fishing trawlers dumping their muck on the way round to the harbour. Then he says, 'I reckon they must have been on a boat out at sea and the mum was holding the kiddy only he struggled and fell, then she dived in after him, but couldn't swim so they drownded.'

'Yeah,' I says, 'or maybe somebody pushed them? Being tied to-gether like.'

But Jimmy thumps me on the arm and says I got too much 'magi-nation.

That night, but, we were still scared. I kept seeing them lying there, the little kid with his eyes wide open. It took me ages to get to sleep. Jimmy, too.

Constable Carter: On 9 May, I had just started my shift when we re-ceived a call at the station that a woman and child had been found washed up on Brighton Beach. It's not a popular spot. The only ap-proach is through a large sandstone opening and the area's full of rocks. The only access is over them.

Constable Flecker and I arrived at the scene to find the woman lying on the sand on her left side with the body of a deceased child, on his right, facing her. Both were above the high tide mark. The child's head looked rather large to me, which I took to be swelling due to drowning, his having been in the water for some time. He was small for his age, pale, wearing short pants and a jumper. I thought at first the woman had also drowned, but it turned out she was still alive, though weak and her breathing very faint. She was of medium height, with a pale complexion, light brown hair, wearing a thin cotton dress in a faded floral print but no shoes. An overcoat was buttoned around both of them, fastened by a belt.

Two local boys, Lenny Duff and Jimmy Nelson found the pair at about seven a.m. and raised the alarm. They were still on the beach when we arrived and I was a bit concerned they might have interfered with the bodies, but they appeared to be undisturbed and the bag Duff showed us only contained shells and other rubbish they'd collected. The woman had nothing of value on her person or anything to identify her. We continued to search the area for evidence but, finding none, we returned to the station where I wrote my report.

Walter Sanders, Ambulance Officer: On Saturday last, I accompanied two constables to the beach, where I examined the body of the deceased, Jack Bryant, and his mother. They were lying on the sand not far from the water's edge. The deceased was under a coat close to his mother, who was still breathing, but her condition was very low. There are rocks at the south-east end of the beach, about sixty yards from where they were found and in my opinion, if they entered the water from rocks on the northern side, they could not have been washed up where they were found.

Dr Gordon: At about eight thirty a.m. on Saturday, an ambulance brought a woman and child to my surgery. The boy was about five years old and already dead, his clothing was covered in wet sand and I estimated he'd been in the water for about two hours. The mother was in an exhausted and weak condition and appeared quite thin, compared to the child. Her clothing was also caked in sand, which suggests she'd been in the water for the same length of time. Neither showed any signs of injury.

I saw to it she had a dry change of clothes and insisted she eat something, but no sooner had she revived a little than she startled me by saying, 'It's my fault. I walked into the water with him.' She claimed to remember nothing more until she found herself washed up on the beach, which I believe to be consistent with her condition at the time.

Once I'd finished examining them, they were taken to the District Hospital, where she was admitted, and the child's body was delivered to the morgue for an autopsy.

Nurse Thomas, District Hospital: She was a strange little woman, very quiet. She appeared in a world of her own, but we all knew what she'd done. It was right round the hospital in minutes. Terrible thing. Her own flesh and blood. And what an odd place to choose, but maybe that was why. Because it was quiet and no one would see her and, now I come to think of it, there's that little cave nearby. Maybe she was planning to take shelter in that? Lots of people living in caves these days. She must have been desperate, poor thing, but she didn't look the criminal type to me, she was too skinny and weak. Still, you never know, it takes all sorts. The whole time she was here, there was a policeman posted outside her door.

Constable McKenzie: On 9 May, I was sent to the District Hospital to guard a patient under arrest. When questioned by staff, the woman gave her name as Minnie May Davis and said she was thirty years old and she lived in Surry Hills.

She said, 'I don't want anyone to know where I'm from or what I've done.'

But later, she gave another name and address, this time in Glebe, which I believe to be the correct one.

She was quite frank about what had happened. 'I'm sorry I made a mess of it,' she said. 'He's dead. I knew soon as we were washed up. Now I suppose I'll be charged with his murder, but I don't care. I'll take what's coming to me. I just don't want anyone knowing what happened.'

Later, I was with her in the hospital morgue and asked her, 'Is this the body of your son you allege you walked into the water with?'

'Yes,' she said.

Then, on Monday 11 May, I went with her to the police station and formally charged her with the murder of Jack Bryant. She said nothing when cautioned, so I asked if she was prepared to tell me what actually happened on the previous Friday night.

'I came down from Sydney,' she said, 'meaning to kill myself and him. I was tired of everything. I had no money, no job and, even if I had, I couldn't take him with me. So I went out on the rocks and walked in. I was under water a long time and don't remember much. I don't want to give any trouble. I've given enough already and if I'd finished it, there wouldn't have been any.'

She showed no remorse but agreed to make a statement which was typed at her dictation and, once read, she signed and stated it as correct.

She was charged with having feloniously and maliciously murdered Jack Bryant aged five and was placed on remand until 25 May. Sergeant Pym made it clear that if she'd applied for bail, it would be opposed. For certain serious offences, unless the accused can establish there are exceptional circumstances, or show cause why their detention is unjustified, bail is denied. Bryant didn't qualify on either ground.

Herbert Jenkins, Undertaker: I was engaged by the police to bury a child not from these parts but who'd been drowned in suspicious circumstances. His mother was from Sydney and an autopsy had been performed, and the body cleared for burial.

Normally, when I arrange a child's funeral, I approach the parents cautiously, avoiding phrases like 'It's God's plan' or 'You'll meet again, someday.' I feel they don't comfort parents, but in this case, I didn't even meet the mother. She was already in police custody charged with his murder.

Who'll Make his Shroud?
I, said the Beetle,

126

With my thread and needle,
I'll make his shroud.

It meant the child would have no one present and a pauper's grave, his mother being penniless, and money for the funeral would have to come from a police fund for the purpose.

Who'll Carry his Coffin?
I, said the Kite,
If it be in the night,
I'll carry his coffin.

On Monday 11 May, I accompanied the body to the Church of England section of Wollongong Cemetery, Rev. Edgar Walker officiating. A small grave was waiting in a remote, grassy corner where there were no headstones. Two gravediggers, John Hansen and Martin Rood, stood by to act as witnesses.

Who'll Dig his Grave?
I, said the Owl,
With my spade and trowel,
I'll dig his grave.

Rev. Walker read a brief version of the burial service, quoting Luke 18:16, 'Jesus called them unto him, and said, "Suffer little children to come unto me, and forbid them not: for such is the kingdom of God."'

Who'll be the Parson?
I, said the Rook,
With my little book,
I'll be the Parson.

When the coffin was lowered, Rev. Walker picked up the first clod, then I did, and as I sprinkled the earth, I felt glad I'd decided to dispense with a shroud as unfeeling, and had dressed the child in clothes our youngest had outgrown and placed an old toy rabbit in his arms. I've dealt with a number of children's burials over the years, mostly from disease or accident but this has to be one of the saddest. Rev. Walker was also moved and told me he'd offered to see the mother in custody, to pray with her, but she'd refused.

Since there was to be no headstone, I made a note of the area to ask the gardeners to plant some flowers nearby. Something bright and cheerful that a child would like.

Sergeant Pym: This has been a dreadful and unnatural crime, that has produced a horrified reaction. The idea that a mother could take the life of her only child is beyond belief. It's hard to imagine a worse act or one that could inspire more public hatred.

And from what I've seen, Bryant has shown no remorse. If anything, it's almost been a sense of relief to her. Her main concern seems to be her bungled suicide, not that she murdered her son. She talks of struggling in the water, knowing the boy was dead before she reached the beach and collapsed.

We would have allowed her to attend the boy's funeral, but she didn't want to, which in my opinion only makes it worse, as if she cared nothing for him.

The newspapers have been quick to pick up the story and embroider it, as they always do. They claim the pair were found by a 'man and boy'. That she left Sydney 'on the five o'clock train'. That she planned to commit suicide and went onto the beach 'near the small lighthouse', wrapped a cloak round the boy imprisoning his arms, and then jumped. Other papers describe her as floating, getting frightened and struggling and big waves carrying them into shore. By that time, the child was dead, and she spent the rest of the night on the beach, but if Dr Gordon is correct, they were only in the water about two hours, which would make it eight p.m. and high tide wasn't till one twenty-seven a.m. Besides, the constables didn't think their clothing was wet enough for them to have been in the water several hours, even if it had dried out a little on the sand.

She is unmarried of course, with no one to help support her and the child, and she says she has no money, so she couldn't have bought train tickets. But she still could have come to us for help. Police don't only evict people when they can't pay the rent, we also help those in need. Last week, for instance, we handed out food relief vouchers at Port Kembla RSL. There were so many people wanting them we ran out and had to call for more to be sent from Wollongong. For a while, things were quite heated and unpleasant and we ended up with a riot on our hands. There were twenty police armed with batons facing a mob of eight hundred angry people. Both sides sustained injuries, police and civilians alike, and six arrests were made, but now the minister's accusing us of being callous in dealing with the unemployed and homeless and he's taken supervision away from us and given it to local committees.

Perhaps Bryant was too proud to ask for help, but she's not the only one doing it tough these days. We have homeless camps all round here. Surely one of them would have taken her in? Anyway, she's in custody now and will be transferred to Long Bay Women's tomorrow.

Policewoman Murphy: I was ordered to escort Bryant down to Wollongong Coroner's Court. We're told not to make friends with prisoners in case they try and put one over us, but I knew she wouldn't be violent. Still, I had to make sure she didn't bolt.

We were to go by the earliest train, so it was barely light when we left Long Bay Gaol for Central. On the way, we had to pass Happy Valley, or maybe it was Hill 60 or Frog Hollow, I can't tell one homeless camp from another, they're all depressing – tents for new arrivals, tin shacks and humpies for those who've been there longer and kids running round everywhere, barefoot, even in winter. But the saddest of all are the women, old and toothless before their time, trying to make the most of it, sharing cooking fires and whatever else they can. Neither of us said a word as we passed, but I could feel Bryant shiver beside me. On the train while we sat together, I undid the cuffs, until she needed to go to the toilet, then I went and stood outside the door.

What struck me was how quiet she was throughout. Most prisoners like to talk, especially those on remand. They'll tell you their life history and, of course, they're always innocent, but Bryant was different, said hardly a word. Nothing about her son, her past life or how it happened. Just stared out the window at passing farms, stretches of bush, or the road.

Deputy Coroner, Mr James Carberry, Coroner's Court, Wollongong, Wednesday 13 May: I conducted a magisterial inquiry into the death of Jack Bryant, aged five, whose dead body was found beside his unconscious mother on Brighton Beach on 9 May.

The child's mother, Katherine Mary Bryant, was in court, having been brought down from Long Bay Women's Gaol. She was a pale, slightly built woman, with light brown hair and grey eyes.

Mr Strom appeared for Bryant, Sergeant Pym represented the police.

Dr John Kent, pathologist, told the court he had performed an autopsy on the body of Jack Bryant on 10 May, at the District Hospital. 'The child was in a fairly well-nourished condition and I saw no marks of violence on him. In my opinion, his death was caused by drowning.' When asked to comment on the child's mother, he replied, 'She appeared to be clear – mentally.'

Matron Casey, Queen Victoria Home for Mothers and Babies: I have known the defendant, Katherine Mary Bryant, for five years. The home was established to give hope and a second chance to women society had shunned. Unmarried mothers. 'Fallen' women, if you like.

These women aren't charged for their stay but are expected to attend to the needs of married women up until the time their own babies are born. After that, they work as domestic servants to pay off their debt to the home.

Bryant was a patient in April 1925 when her baby was born. She remained until 18 June, the following year. It's a small home and most of the mothers leave soon after their babies are born, but Bryant stayed longer, because she had nowhere else to go. She's from England and has no relatives in Australia, so she was grateful for a place to stay. She kept working as a domestic while her son was still a baby and during that time, I had plenty of opportunity to form an opinion of her character and found her to be a good, hard-working, honest girl.

Unmarried mothers' babies are mostly put up for adoption, because their mothers can't look after them and adoption is better than sending them to an orphanage. We ask married mothers to express extra milk, which is collected each day by a 'milk train' and taken to Camperdown Hospital for these babies until they're old enough to go to their new parents. But in Katherine's case, adoption wasn't going to be possible. From the time he was born, her baby was different from others and no couple would have wanted him. He was always crying and fretful, very hard to settle and, to tell you the truth, he looked a bit odd to me. I don't think he was quite – normal.

I kept in touch with her for about three years after she left the home, and even by then Jack still couldn't speak, not properly. And he had an unusually large head for a child his age, so he tended to stand out from other children. Of course, I did what I could to see she was placed in suitable positions, in situations where she could have the boy with her, but after a couple of years, I lost track of her and didn't see her again until last Saturday, in Long Bay Gaol.

It was there she told me she had no money, but was afraid to ask the state for help, knowing they'd probably take the boy from her. He was all she had in the world and she couldn't bear to think of him being in an orphanage. But I must say, she never struck me as the sort of woman who'd do something like this, at least, not deliberately, in a normal state of mind.

Sir, if the state will allow her to go, I will undertake to feed and clothe her until she is able to find work again.

Mrs Molly Kent: I run a boarding house in Glebe and have known Katherine Bryant for about three weeks. She rented a room from me for about that length of time and was there until 8 May.

She left on the Friday morning with her son, Jack, saying she was going to stay with relatives in Melbourne. They both seemed in good health and spirits, and not worried about anything, but she was always a private person and never said much. She certainly didn't mention any money problems. Sometimes, she'd ask for needle and thread to mend their clothes, especially if she was going for a job, and once I gave her some spare wool and she knitted a jumper for him and with what was left over, a toy squirrel she stuffed with rags. I remember her saying squirrels reminded her of England. Anyway, the child adored it and carried it round with him everywhere. I used to see him out the garden on the grass beside the flower beds, hugging it.

I didn't see her again until 10 May at the hospital, where I was shown the boy's body and identified him as her son, Jack Bryant. The child was deficient in his speech and, to be honest, I thought he was a bit simple, though, of course, I never said as much. When I asked why she'd done it, all she said was, 'I don't know. I'm sorry for what I've done, and I'll miss poor Jack.'

I asked why she hadn't said she needed money. She could have stayed on a bit longer till she was more settled. But she didn't want to do that. She said I'd been good to her and she wouldn't have been able to repay me.

She always struck me as a sensible young woman. I can't imagine why she would want to drown herself and her little boy.

Harry Myles, boarding house resident: She was a pleasant little woman, but hard-up, like the rest of us. She saw me repairing a pair of shoes once, I have a last and do all my own mending, and she asked if I could fix hers and the kiddy's, but I might have to wait a bit till she could pay me. I told her I didn't want anything, I was happy to help. The last time I saw her was on the Thursday and she seemed bright enough, but then she usually was. Always had a friendly word for everyone. She told me she was going to Melbourne to find work, because she couldn't get a job in Sydney even though she'd tried, and I know she had, poor thing. I used to see her set out each day, but she never had much luck.

She was a good mother, I'll say that for her, lavished affection on that boy of hers. It was lovely to see them together, they were so close, though he didn't seem quite right to me. Can't quite put me finger on it. She can't have been married, or maybe divorced, because when she went for jobs, she always had to have him with her, and with so many out of work, employers can pick and choose, and not have to take on kiddies as well.

He wasn't a bad little fellow, even though we couldn't get a word out of him, but soon as he saw her, his face would light up. I never talked to the other lodgers about him, but I always thought he'd be a right handful as he got older.

On the Thursday night, she packed a suitcase and said goodbye to us, saying she'd be heading off early next morning. Of course, none of us had any idea such an awful thing would happen. It's been a terrible shock. She just didn't seem the kind of woman who'd harm anybody.

Mrs Alice Walters, former employer: Some of us whom Bryant had worked for took the trouble to write to the Prisoners' Aid Society saying she was a good woman, industrious, and of good character. She moved jobs quite a bit, but we all gave her good references. Her problem was the child. She was clearly devoted to him, but with no one to mind him while she worked, she had to have him with her, and he was difficult, to say the least. He followed her everywhere, constantly getting under-foot. On one occasion, she was scrubbing my kitchen floor. It's linoleum, black and white squares, so it shows every mark, and some-how, he'd managed to get hold of a ladle and was walking behind her pouring dirty water from the bucket all over the floor she'd just scrubbed. She didn't lose her temper – I would have – but she didn't say a word, just took the ladle from him and turned round, and began scrubbing the whole lot again. But to be perfectly blunt, the last thing you need in a kitchen is a child getting in the way. It could be danger-ous. And he had this nasty habit of suddenly appearing behind her whenever she brought in the tea tray. In front of guests, too. At one of my bridge parties, he stood staring at the ladies and I could tell they felt uncomfortable.

But the last straw came that time with Ruth, my youngest. I'd managed to persuade Katherine to let him outside to play with Ruth in the garden, so she could get on with her work unhindered, but for some strange reason, he began picking all my pansies and lining them up in rows. Ruth told him it was naughty and tried to stop him, but he burst out laughing, maniacally, and Ruth was terrified, poor child, she's only four. She didn't know how to stop him, and his laughter grew louder and louder till he ended up lying on the ground clutching his stomach. That's when Ruth picked up a handful of soil and dropped it in his open mouth. To stop him. She was crying when I ran out, 'Mummy, Mummy, make him stop!' It hadn't done him any harm that I could see, and nothing would have come of it, apart from cleaning him up, but Katherine had seen it all from the kitchen window. She rushed out and told Ruth she was a cruel little girl and took him inside. After that, we agreed it would be best if she found another position.

Mr Strom, counsel for the defendant: Miss Bryant's character references attest to her being honest and hard-working and she impressed me as being of good character, although perhaps a bit simple-minded, since she doesn't fully appear to realise what has happened. However, she's been truthful in her replies and hasn't tried to evade my questions and, if she doesn't seem overly upset, we must remember that adversity and trouble can upset a woman's nervous system, even her mental balance.

When Miss Bryant first regained consciousness and spoke to Dr Gordon, I don't believe her words were callously meant. She was clearly not as well-nourished as her child, which would suggest she made sure he was fed at her expense. The clothing of both was damp when they were found, but not very wet, implying that they had been out of the water for some time, so the child probably died soon after entering the water.

Miss Bryant did not strike me as a woman with criminal intent. She clearly loved her child and would not have acted as she did if her mind had been in a normal state. It was her great fear of being left destitute and separated from him that made her behave so desperately.

Deputy Coroner Mr James Carberry, Coroner's Court, Wednesday 13 May: Throughout proceedings, the accused never once spoke or looked towards the bench. Instead, she concentrated her gaze on the ceiling of the courtroom, while playing with her hands, not engaging with anyone present.

Having heard the evidence and listened to the police statements and character witnesses, my finding is that the child, Jack Bryant, met his death by drowning, wilfully inflicted. Accordingly, his mother Katherine Mary Bryant is to be returned to Long Bay Women's Gaol on remand until 25 May, and is committed to stand trial

Policewoman Murphy: On the way back, after she'd been charged, she seemed to change. If anything, she was a little brighter. She said, 'I'm glad it's over. It's a relief. Now I can face whatever's left for me,' then she clammed up again.

It was dark when we got back to Long Bay and I saw her through the gates into the care of warders. I was worried how some of the other prisoners might treat her, whether they'd attack her for what she'd done, so I said, 'Goodbye, Bryant. Look after yourself and good luck for the trial.'

She nodded and gave me her only smile of the day.

George Thompson, truck driver: It was the missus made me pick them up. Gladys sometimes calls me hard-hearted and unfeeling, but I prefer to think I'm just wary. It pays to be, what with so many homeless wandering the roads these days. They may be down on their luck, but who's to say they don't have a kitchen knife or screwdriver handy to stick in your ribs and rob you. Gladys never worries about such things. She thinks the best of everyone, but I tell her there's lots more crime about now, so you need to be on your guard.

Gladys Thompson, wife of the above: George usually needs a bit of a prod before he does anything. He's not a bad man, but he can be stubborn as a clam at times and I couldn't bear to leave them there. She wasn't hitching a ride, but the poor thing was struggling with that suitcase and the kiddie screaming to be picked up. He looked too big for her to carry any distance, she seemed so thin, and I remember thinking, how's she's going to manage with him and the bag? So I told George to pull over.

'Would you like a lift, love?' I asked. 'You look done in and we're heading towards Wollongong if that's any use.'

She hesitated a moment, then said, 'Yes. Thanks. Come on, Jack.'

There was no room in the cabin for them, so she hoisted the case up into the tray, lifted the kiddy in and climbed up after him. I didn't get a real good look at them, but as we drove off, I could see through the back window she was cuddling him and he'd stopped grizzling.

It was late afternoon, around five, when we left them by the roadside. 'Will you be all right, dear? Where are you headed?'

'Melbourne,' she said, and I said, 'Oh dear, you should have caught the train, love. It'll take you weeks on foot.'

Next day, George went out to the truck and found the suitcase, but by then I thought she'd be much further on. Not that there was anything in it, really. Nothing to say who she was, just a few clothes for him and a toy squirrel, hand-knitted, with odd button eyes.

Then, on Monday morning, George took it to the police station and came home with this funny look on his face. 'You and your ideas!' he said. 'A fine one she turned out to be!'

'Who?'

'That woman with the kid you made me pick up. Wish I hadn't now. Just goes to show, you can't trust anyone these days.'

Of course, I refused to believe him at first. It wasn't till he showed me the newspaper and then I felt terrible. We should have done more for them. Not less. Tried to help them somehow. That poor little mite. We should have offered them a bed for the night, or a meal, but George said, 'Gladys, we did our bit. We can't go helping every stranger wandering the road.'

Governor, Long Bay Women's Gaol: Katherine Bryant was held on remand here for some months. Such prisoners are kept separate from other inmates and treated differently. They're allowed to wear civilian clothing and take phone calls from their lawyers, being considered innocent until proved guilty, but in Bryant's case she'd already confessed.

Despite the appalling nature of her crime, she showed no signs of violence while here, but remained quiet and withdrawn. You would never have guessed she was capable of such a thing. She answered the warders when spoken to, and gave no trouble, but she felt she was watched the whole time and she'd rather be left alone. We pointed out this was not a hotel but a gaol. What she wanted was of no concern to us.

Dr Hargreaves, visiting doctor, Long Bay Gaol: I examined the prisoner on several occasions from 12 May on, and my initial concern was that she was undernourished. As to her state of mind, when I asked the usual questions – What year was it? Who was the prime minister? – she was able to answer, 'James Henry Scullin,' when I wouldn't have known his middle name. She remembered the bridge spans had met on 19 August last year, when I wasn't exactly sure, and she seemed fully aware of her surroundings and why she was there. At no stage did she show any remorse for what she'd done, but I cannot be sure if this was due to hardheartedness, or not wanting to show her true feelings. She struck me as a very private person who preferred to keep her thoughts and feelings to herself. I have advised the court that in my opinion she is not insane, and capable of standing trial.

Lennie: Hey, Jimmy! You know that woman and kid we found on the beach?
Jimmy: Yeah.

Lennie: Today's the trial.

Jimmy: But isn't she in gaol already?

Lennie: Yeah, but Mum says she still has to go to court.

Jimmy: Well, she didn't look like a murderer to me. She was too skinny.

Lennie: They're not all big and fat, but.

Jimmy: Yeah, well, maybe she wasn't quite right in the head. Like, if she wanted to, she could have jumped off The Gap any time and left the kid.

Mr Robert Macleay, KC, Crown Prosecutor, Central Criminal Court, Thursday 24 September, 1931: Since she's English, Bryant may not have known the Criminal Court. It's an impressive building, stone, with columns and portico for those on the right side of the law, but in her case the Black Maria bringing her from Long Bay would have driven round the back and she would have been kept in a holding cell until called.

I watched her step into the dock and wondered what she made of us all in gowns and wigs, but if anything, she only appeared slightly embarrassed, perhaps at all the fuss she's caused.

I always try and make an effort with my appearance. I keep my wig in good trim and my papers neatly stacked, and once the prisoner is in the dock, I try and avoid all eye contact with them, preferring instead to look to the judge or jury. But in this case, Bryant was doing the avoiding. She didn't look once in my direction, nor at the bench. She didn't even appear to look at the jury, but instead sat with downcast eyes the whole time and I remember thinking she's not doing herself any favours. She was coming across as callous.

It is a sad case, but she is fit to stand and will be represented. Mr Strom being based in Wollongong, he has arranged for Mr Clarence to appear, pro bono.

Mr Clarence, for the Defence: Macleay presented a strong case, as you'd expect. Murder is murder. So it was up to me to tug at the jury's heart strings. A mother, no help, no prospects, so I was hoping, when they retired, that I'd have it in the bag. But they were out for two hours and I began to get a bit nervous. I didn't think she deserved to hang, but you never can tell how a jury will react.

Jury Foreman: Guilty. On the grounds of Temporary Insanity.

Mr Clarence: Well, Bryant, you must be pleased. The jury was on our side.

Bryant: What's it mean, what the judge said?

Mr Clarence: Kept in custody, at the Governor's Pleasure? It means you'll be sent to an asylum.

Bryant: But I'm not mad. That's not what I wanted. I thought they'd hang me and be done with it, then I'd have been with Jack.

Clarence: No, believe me, in the circumstances, this is the best outcome, and what I was hoping for. You don't deserve to hang, the judge knows that, and so does the jury, but he also knows it would be worse sending you back to Long Bay.

Bryant: Why?

Clarence: Because the other inmates would take it out on you for killing Jack. They always do. Sooner or later, you'd be bashed. And more than once.

Bryant: But how long will I have to stay in the asylum?

Clarence: It's hard to say. Years probably. Until the doctors decide you're no longer a danger to yourself or others.

Matron Baxter: She seemed a mere slip of a thing standing in my office that first day, but I was firm with her. 'Well, Bryant, you're here for as long as it suits them,' I told her, 'so if you know what's good for you, you'll follow the rules and won't cause trouble.'

I saw to it she was given a uniform, the plain, grey dress all the women wear, and gave orders she was to be put in a room by herself that first night. Dr Milson would see her next morning, but till then she was to have meals by herself, and after lights out, I made sure she was checked on regularly to see she settled and did no harm to herself. It's only a small room, with a barred window too high up for her to see out. This is so they are kept quiet and aren't distracted. The beds have straps attached as a precaution but, in Bryant's case, I felt fairly sure they wouldn't be necessary.

During the night, she was seen crying, but whether from remorse or her new surroundings, I can't say. She was also restless, but that may have been because she was finding it noisy after Long Bay. We have patients who call out at night. They wail and scream, some of them. The wilder ones especially are always more noisy after dark. She was observed finally falling asleep hugging her pillow and at one point, perhaps because she felt she was being watched, she pulled the blanket up over her head and stayed like that for the rest of the night.

Dr Milson, psychiatrist: Women have always been the weaker sex, closer to nature, their biological characteristics more attuned to the rhythms of their natural cycles, in particular to motherhood. Their nervous systems are more sensitive than men's, which means they are more easily upset, so stress, such as desertion by a husband, can be a definite trigger to female insanity. It can cause them to become withdrawn, even to the point of catatonia.

The basic wage for women is £1/19/0, but as a domestic servant Bryant would have earned less, the amount being determined by their employer, who may well have charged board for her and the child as well. Once that income was gone, the pressure of caring for her child without the support of a male breadwinner would be enough to have her incarcerated, even without the added complication of murder.

The most common motive for filicide-suicide is an attempt by the parent to relieve any real or imagined suffering on the part of their child. We call this altruistic filicide.

Matron Baxter: After that first night, she was put into a ward with other inmates, but she complained of being unable to sleep, because one or two of the patients kept coming up to her bed and staring, which she found frightening. I told her she'd have to get used to it, they were only curious, and eventually they would leave her alone.

Dr Milson: I saw Bryant the morning after her admission and initially she refused to answer any of my questions till I pointed out that I had all the time in the world, years if necessary, so it was in her best interests to answer. She is not catatonic, but seems acutely depressed and admits to feeling low, and has done, not just for weeks or months, but years. Ever since she left the Queen Victoria Home.

When I asked her about Jack, she said he was a lovely baby, even though for a long time he didn't smile like others, nor do any of the things they could, and he cried a lot, which got her down.

She told me she believed he had very few chances in life and, as she saw it, killing him and then herself was the kindest option, indeed her only option. She said his head always seemed too big for his body and she used to wonder if this were her fault, that perhaps she'd done something while she was carrying him to cause that and it made her feel guilty, for bringing him into the world. She had tried to create a space, a cocoon to protect him, but at the same time she felt trapped, as if in a long dark tunnel from which she could never escape.

Matron Baxter: Some of the inmates here hardly speak at all. They might mutter or let out a scream that can scare the life out of you till you get used to it. At mealtimes, they either toy with their food or sit shovelling it into their mouths, spoon after spoon, like machines, till their bowl's empty. Porridge, mush, anything. Mud, if they weren't watched.

Then there are those who can't or won't feed themselves. They're made to sit on benches arranged in a square, facing out, waiting for the nurse to come round and stick a spoonful of stew in their mouths, one at a time, and when she comes back, they're supposed to have swallowed, but some of them gag, or spit it out, which can be very frustrating. They can't help it, but honestly, they're like naughty children at times. The food, I admit, is not very imaginative, but it's wholesome. We grow whatever vegetables we can, chokos, pumpkin, Queensland Blues mostly, which tend to drown out the taste of potato which they like more, and if we can manage to get any, we add a little mince as well. Nothing that requires a knife or fork, since they would be dangerous, then it's all mashed up so they can't choke on it. Sometimes instead of stew they get soup made from cabbages and turnips from the garden.

Bryant is definitely the odd one out. She's clearly depressed and probably bored, after all, she has nothing to do all day but wait to see Dr Milson.

Dr Milson, psychiatrist: Did anyone tell you to kill Jack?

Bryant: No. He was a child.

Dr Milson: But did you hear voices? Ordering you?

Bryant: No. There were times I asked God why He'd done this to me, but voices, no. And one time when things were really bad, I thought of taking him to the Easter Show and losing him. Others have done it. Taken their kids to Sideshow Alley and distracted them while they disappear. They get taken to the Lost Children's tent and in two days, if nobody turns up to collect them, they become wards of the state. But I couldn't do that to Jack. Anyway, where was I going to find money to go to the show?

Dr Milson: Have you ever tried to kill yourself before?

Bryant: No. But I've thought about it. Jumping from the Harbour Bridge, perhaps. After all, enough men have fallen from it. But how would I get up there and what would happen to Jack? An orphanage for sure, and how would he cope? There were other times I told myself that once his body started to grow, his head wouldn't seem so large, that somehow he'd seem more in proportion. I even reminded myself that

Dr Bradfield was short with a big head but that hadn't stopped him designing the bridge and for a while I stopped worrying. But Jack still didn't talk – well, hardly, not enough that others could understand him – and he didn't behave like other children his age. So it finally dawned on me he was never going to change, no matter what I did and I was a bad mother for wanting him to.

Dr Milson: Initially, she had nothing much to do with the other patients. I was told she avoided them at mealtimes and sat at one end of one of the long tables, not speaking, and during the day she kept mostly to herself.

Matron Baxter: It did take time, but gradually she started to settle in more. One day, she saw one of the cleaners in the corridor with a mop and bucket and offered to help and when I asked why she'd offered, she said, 'Because it will stop me thinking. I can't sit staring into space.'

Of course, in Long Bay she would have been put to work in the kitchen or laundry, but here most of the patients can't be relied on to undertake tasks if left to themselves. But she has always worked, so to her it means regularity. Security in a way, a comfort of sorts. So I asked could she sew, because we have a sewing room.

'Sew? What?' she asked.

I told her we needed sheets mended, swapping outsides for thin middles and we could always do with more uniforms for the women, sometimes even shrouds. She went pale at this and said she couldn't face shrouds, but for the rest, yes. So we put her to work and she proved most willing. She could turn a seam as neat as any of the nurses and often faster.

Dr Milson: With no family here, did you ever think of going back to England?

Bryant: Yes, but how? I'd no money and no prospects back there. Only family. And they might not have wanted me. I realise if I'd stayed in

England, none of this would have happened. But then I wouldn't have had Jack, either.

Dr Milson: So, when were you born?

Bryant: 1900, in Wolverhampton. I had a brother Harold, four years older, and a sister Lily, two years older. Pa worked in a factory making engineering tools, but when I was still quite small, we moved to London, because he'd heard talk his factory might close. He'd had this fear of the workhouse ever since he was a kid, but in London, he found another job in another factory. When war broke out, Pa was fifty-seven and too old but his factory started making gun parts, so his job was secure. Our Harold was eighteen and couldn't wait. He was just over five foot three, but a bit pale and fresh-faced, so he turned up to Recruitment with coal dust smeared round his jaw so he'd look like he hadn't shaved. When he told Ma he'd been accepted, she nearly died. Her only son off to fight the Hun and Pa had signed the papers! He said they wouldn't send him overseas till he turned nineteen, but Harold had said he was nineteen already and that did it. Ma made him promise not to try anything silly and he laughed and said the extra money would come in handy, with one less mouth to feed. Ration posters were up already saying if you added up all the slices of bread wasted, there'd be enough to fill two whole ships. Waste any, and you were helping the German navy blockade us. At first, the government said no to women working – middle-class women, that is. Working-class girls went into domestic service, or factories, soon as we left school.

Dr Milson: Did you feel you were doing something worthwhile?

Bryant: I suppose. With the men away, there were all sorts of jobs; tram fare collecting, sticking up billposters, delivering letters and telegrams. But factories too were turning out machines and parts, even aeroplanes, and needed all the workers they could get. Then, as more men went to the Front, more of us took their jobs.

Lily was working as a machinist in a textile factory and I'd started as a tidy-upper, having just left school, but our factory switched to making uniforms, and we did that till someone tipped us off about munitions. Then Lily, bold as a brass knob, told them she was eighteen, and said I was sixteen and factories weren't too fussy. 'Sides, we didn't mind getting out of bed before five while it was still dark and walking to work. They started us off on a lathe, seven-foot long, me in my blouse and long skirt, but after a couple of days my eyes were that bad with grit they sent me to hospital to have my eyeballs scraped and after that, they put me on cartridges. Then one of the girls said you got extra for filling shells. So we put our hands up, even though it was dirty and we had to wear overalls, brown so as not to show the dirt, and belted in, with trousers underneath and our hair covered with mobcaps.

Dr Milson: So it was more dangerous?

Bryant: Too right. Picric acid. Big clumps of poisonous yellow crystals. The factory called them 'HE shells' and must have thought we were stupid if we couldn't figure out HE meant high explosive and all the while they kept telling us we'd be fine as long as we kept our wits about us. So we stuck it out, dirt and noise till we felt we'd go deaf, all for £2.4s.6d, more than we'd ever seen, but it didn't seem fair doing the same work as men only they got more. Factory owners could pay us whatever they liked. Then tram conductresses went on strike for better wages, and some munitions workers in other factories, only we were scared of putting the Munitions Tribunal offside and we'd lose our jobs. In the end, it made no difference.

Dr Milson: You were still helping the war effort.

Bryant: Yes. Even though it was dead boring and we tried hard not to think of the thousands who'd be killed because of us. We kept telling ourselves plenty of factories in Germany were making the same kind of shells to kill our boys. But they didn't tell us we'd turn yellow. Our faces and hands and the stuff made us sneeze and left this nasty, bitter taste in our throats and heaven knows what it did to our innards. There were accidents too that they tried to hush up, and by the end of the war, rumours that maybe four hundred girls had died, but we never knew. We worried what we'd look like when it was all over. Like old crones, because people started calling us 'canaries' on account of how yellow we looked. Some even stood aside in the street, like we were lepers.

Dr Milson: Did you resent that?

Bryant: Of course. Then one night, towards the end, two of the girls asked us to a pub and, not wanting to seem uppity, we said yes and next thing we're settled in a corner where the lighting's dim and these soldiers come in and asked could they join us. Annie says, 'Charmed, I'm sure,' and they seemed nice enough. Colonials. On leave or, as Ma said later, 'Out for a good time.' After a few drinks, we went for a walk. Annie and Edna were bolder than we were. We could hear them laughing and giggling, their chaps' arms round their waists, Lily and me more careful. They only had a week in London and Ma was suspicious, saying she had a sixth sense about these things, but Pa said, 'Go and have some fun, there's precious little around.'

Reggie was Australian, younger and taller than the others and a bit of a clown with red hair and always making us laugh, and I liked him, probably because he didn't call me canary. He said I looked tanned like I'd been in Australia and what if I wasn't a pink English rose, I was his golden wattle. It was blarney, but it made me feel good and at seventeen, as I was by then, you need that. So I saw him most days till their leave was up. Not that Reg didn't try it on still, so Ma was right. She used to say by the time their hand got from your hem to your knee you knew what they had in mind, but he was quite blunt, saying, 'Aw, come on, love, you wouldn't send a bloke back to the Front without a bit, would you?' and the thing was, part of me felt grown-up enough to say yes, but I knew I'd cop it if Ma found out, so I sent him packing. He wrote, after the Armistice, saying he'd been kept back in France digging graves and was I married, engaged or did I have a feller? He was hoping to get over to London before he was shipped home, but I never heard from him again and part of me was glad nothing come of it.

Dr Milson: And after the War?

Bryant: It affected us badly. Harold was killed in '16, and Ma and Pa never got over it, and. I realised then what it must be to lose a child. Even a grown one. They moped around all day, hardly saying a word, even when the Armistice was signed and the rest of the country went mad. Big Ben chimed for the first time since it started. Shops and schools closed and everyone poured out on the streets to join in. We left the factories in our overalls, waving flags, banging tin trays, scaring the bad times away, but so many families had lost a husband, son, or brother. And those who came back had eyepatches, or sleeves pinned up, their lungs done in from gas or nerves like jelly. Violent too, some of them, to their families, when the grog was in them especially, but they drank to forget.

Dr Milson: None of us knew what to expect.

Bryant: We felt washed-up. Rubbish on a beach.

Dr Milson: How did you cope?

Bryant: My eyes were sore still and the whites yellow and my skin felt itchy a lot of the time. I'd get these niggardly headaches and dizziness too, but the itchy skin and headaches they said would pass.

Dr Milson: And did you find other work?

Bryant: Me and Lily tried other factories but none of them wanted us with the men back. Then Pa had his accident. His factory was making engineering tools again, and maybe he'd become a bit careless, but one day he lost two fingers, and after that, he couldn't work.

Dr Milson: So how did you manage?

Bryant: Ma let a room. Our house had only small bedrooms but Harold's old room Pa painted with a brush tied to his hand. Rooms were in demand with men wanting digs, so it was snapped up and Lily and me took in washing and mending, and Pa potted about fixing things, broken chairs and the like, with his left hand and he started a vegie garden out the back. William our lodger had a limp and climbed the stairs slowly but he was becoming sweet on Lily and she on him and Ma was delighted at the thought of maybe having a daughter married, but it made me realise I had to make a life of my own.

So one night, must have been in 1920, when William and Lily were out and the three of us were sitting round the table after tea, I told them I was thinking of emigrating, to New Zealand or Canada, even Australia, and they looked shocked. It was blunt, but I said I'd a little saved from munitions, and there didn't seem much point staying in England where I had no future. I tried softening it a bit saying once Lily and William were married and in a place of their own and me gone, they'd have two rooms to let. I even joked, 'Who knows? I might even find a husband in Australia! There's not enough to go round here.' They were quiet for a bit, then Ma said perhaps it was for the best, but Pa was upset, his only son gone and soon both his daughters. So I hugged him and said I still loved him and Ma made us another cup of tea, then he felt better. 'Australia would be the warmest,' he said and we all laughed. It was true I had a bit of money but not enough for the whole fare, so I took a berth travelling steerage with the chance to work part of my passage.

Shipping News: Miss Katherine Bryant to Sydney. Domestic, age twenty. Aberdeen Line – *Themistocles* – 3rd Class.

Dr Milson: And when was this?

Bryant: 20 January 1921 we sailed, arrived 8 March. Mind you, when I saw the cabin with its porthole barely above the waterline I had second thoughts, but by then it was too late. Ma was hugging me and insisting I take her lucky Queen Victoria shilling, and they were calling for all visitors ashore. Four of us were sharing, berths both sides and hardly room to move, so we took turns sitting on the lower bunks. The other girls left the ship in Melbourne hoping for factory work but promised to keep in touch, and they did for a while. I chose Sydney because Reggie had talked about it. Not that I had any idea if he was still there or how to contact him, but it seemed as good a place as any to start a new life.

One of the crew said to try The Rocks for somewhere cheap to rent, and it sounded like it was near a beach, so I was surprised by the narrow streets and little houses that seemed more like London. The landlady eyed me up and down saying, 'No gentlemen callers, or you'll be out on your ear.' But when I asked where could I find an agency placing domestics, she softened a little and directed me up town.

It wasn't long before I found a job five days a week, in a big, old house in Elizabeth Bay, as a maid, since they already had a housekeeper and probably just as well. Her room was scarcely bigger than a broom cupboard and I was glad to come back to my own little room of a night. I had a primus stove for a kettle, a bathroom down the hall and not much cleaning, since I was gone early each morning to catch the tram and it was often dark when I came home. If the family were having company for dinner, I had to stay on to help and I'd miss the last tram and have to walk back to town. I hated those times, with the roads so dark, but I clutched Ma's lucky shilling and stuck to main roads under street lights and I never had much money on me, so not worth robbing.

Dr Milson: Clearly, things didn't stay that way. How did you come to have Jack?

Bryant: I stuck out the job for two years till April of '23, then I decided to try for barmaid and the second pub I tried was prepared to take me on trial. Soon I was pulling taps like I'd been doing it for years, laughing at their jokes, sidestepping their cheek, and if it got too rough, I'd call the manager to sort them out. We had all sorts in, seamen, wharfies, labourers, chippies and builders, and come six o'clock we'd call, 'Time gentleman' and throw them out, which meant I got to go home early, which suited me fine. I'd been working there nearly a year when one afternoon who should walk in but Reggie. Sounds impossible, I know, and I didn't recognise him at first, not out of uniform and more weathered, but his hair, red and curly, you couldn't miss. I could never understand why his mates called him Bluey, especially when they said it was because of his red hair.

Dr Milson: And this was?

Bryant: Must have been early '24. They'd chosen an English company to build the bridge and signed contracts in March of that year, so there seemed to be more going on round The Rocks and more men coming into the pub of an evening. Anyway, he came straight up to the bar and said in a loud voice, 'Well, if it isn't my little wattle, fancy seeing you!' I felt my cheeks start to burn, but he laughed and said, 'You come to Australia to find me, love? Hear that, fellers? This lassie's come all the way from England. She must be sweet on me!' The other blokes started laughing and I'm ready to die. But minutes later they've forgotten, and Reggie says he's never forgotten our time in London and was ever so sad not seeing me before they shipped him home. But now he's the luckiest man in Sydney. Blarney, but the truth of it is, I was pleased to see him. He was something of a link with home and he made me laugh.

Dr Milson: So you began seeing him again?

Bryant: Yes, he was waiting for me outside that night and we walked round the streets, just like in London, and he told me he was a wharfie on the docks, which was good pay.

He walked me back to my boarding house and it was only after I got inside that I realised I'd lost Ma's lucky shilling. It was in my coat pocket and must have been the clink I heard when we stepped off the kerb. Down a drain, probably. I was thinking of writing home to say I'd met Reggie again, but wouldn't mention her shilling. It would only upset her.

From then on, I saw him twice a week, maybe, in the pub. He said he only came to see me, but it was still a while before I agreed to go out with him and then only for a drink. He knew so much about The Rocks, and all the narrow streets where he said plague had broken out and houses and pubs were knocked down. It brought the whole place alive and I found myself looking forward to seeing him of an evening.

Then one night, I suggested we go for a picnic on Saturday or Sunday.

Looking back, he seemed to hesitate, then he said, 'Right you are, but it'll have to be Saturday, Sundays are tied up.'

'You don't strike me as a churchgoing man,' I laughed but he said Sundays he went to see his mum and I thought, 'Now there's a kind man. Not many chaps would.'

So the following Saturday, we went to the Botanic Gardens and I took a picnic. It was a lovely day, warm, and we were there till about five o'clock, when he suddenly jumped up, said he had to go, that he had things to do before seeing his mum next day.

After that, I counted on seeing him most Saturdays and we went to all sorts of places, like Bondi Beach, where he rolled up his trousers and went paddling while I sat on a rug and watched. One day, it was the races, where he won a bit, which made him happy, and all the while he kept saying how wonderful it'd be to spend more time together, all our time in fact, and it made me think he was plucking up courage to propose to me. I even made bold and suggested one Sunday he take me to meet his mum, but he said. 'No,' a bit too quickly, now I think of it, that she was in a home and very frail and he'd have to pick the right time. So I thought no more about it, while he kept telling me how much he loved me, and didn't know what'd he done to deserve me, I was the best thing to happen to him. All that.

Then once it started getting colder, he said why didn't we go to my boarding house for an indoor picnic and I told him my landlady would throw me out if she caught us. But a few weeks later, he took a room in a nearby pub, saying he was tired of catching the train home every night after a heavy shift. He lived in a suburb down south, and really early starts were taking a toll. So next Saturday, we went to his room, where he had nice lunch set out, bread and ham, cheese and apples, and that's where we spent most Saturdays through the winter.

But came the day I realised I'd missed and even then I thought, a day, two days was nothing, it was only when it was a fortnight passed with no sign of him in the pub I began to worry.

Finally, one evening he strolled in, cheeky as always till he sees the look on my face, and says, 'What's up, love? Missed me?'

I was holding a glass in one hand and a tea towel in the other and was tempted to throw one or both at him, but all I said was, 'No, but I want to see you after.'

Then when six o'clock came and they'd swilled their last, I went out to meet him. For a moment, I couldn't see him in the half-light and thought he'd done a runner, but he came out of the shadows saying, 'Sorry I haven't been round much lately, love. I've had a lot to do with Mum.'

'Well, you might have to do a bit for me now, because I'm in the family way.' He stared as if he hadn't heard and maybe it was shock, but I hoped he was pleased. 'What? Lost for words?'

'How long?'

'A month maybe, give or take. But you said you loved me, I was the best thing to happen to you, so can we get married, soon?'

Even under the street light, I could tell he'd gone pale. 'Reggie? You want to marry me, don't you?'

'Yeah, but what I'd like and what's possible are two separate things.'

I had this sudden sick feeling in the pit of my stomach. 'What d'you mean?'

'I'm already married.'

I felt my knees start to give way and would have fainted if he hadn't caught me by the arm.

'You can't be? You said you'd marry me.'

'No, I didn't. I said I'd like to. I'm sorry, love. In England we had a bit of fun, but there was this girl back here, see, she'd knitted socks for me and written letters and Mum said since she'd waited, I couldn't let her down.'

'Did you love her?'

'It's not as simple as that. I was fond of her and now we have two little girls and she had trouble with the second, so she won't be having any more. They're still young too, so I couldn't walk out on them. Besides, she's Catholic, so she'd never give me a divorce.'

I made my way to a bench to sit down. My head was spinning, I needed to think. 'How have you managed to see me all this time?'

'Because I was lying to her and I feel bad about it. I told her I was working late Saturdays, shifts and overtime. But things are a bit tight money-wise and just lately she's been asking about the extra money. Where's it gone?'

'And Sundays?'

'I'm with her and the kids. It's the only time they see me all week.'

'But what about Sundays with your mum?'

'I'm afraid that wasn't true either. She died. Two years ago.'

I didn't know whether I was more angry with him for lying or me for being stupid enough to believe him. 'But what am I meant to do?'

'I don't know. See to it, I suppose. There must be some woman round here who could fix you up. Your landlady might know someone.

'What, and have her throw me out on the street once she finds out, so I have nowhere to go? Thanks a lot.'

Even in the half-light I could see he looked not ashamed so much as embarrassed. All his jokes counted for nothing and I suddenly saw him as pathetic.

'I'll chip in a bit towards it, but I can't manage much.'

I was so angry I could barely speak but heard myself saying, 'I never want to see you again, Reggie. Ever. Don't come anywhere the pub. Find somewhere else to drink.'

And after that, I didn't see him. I don't know what became of him and don't care. Except, I hope he went back to his wife and kids and did the right thing by them. But who knows? Maybe he had somebody else lined up?

Meanwhile, I had to keep working for as long as I could and, as I suspected, once I started to show my landlady wanted me out. Said someone wanted my room, but luckily for me, Ted the publican was kind enough to say I could go on working so long as it didn't show behind the bar and not being tall that helped. And his wife, Dora, took me under her wing and gave me a little back room upstairs and said I could stay for as long as I needed. Then when the time came, she knew the matron at the home. Rather funny, now I think of it, ending up in the Queen Victoria Home, having lost my lucky Queen Victoria shilling.

Dr Milson: But it doesn't explain how you ended up on Brighton Beach.

Bryant: Because I lied to them at the boarding house in Glebe. I couldn't tell them how bad things really were, that I had less than £1, when most of them were pretty skint. I couldn't have taken money from them. Mrs Kent was good to let me stay, on tick, till I found a job, but any longer would have been bludging. Truth is, there were no jobs. At least, none where I could take a kid with me. I told them I had relatives in Melbourne, because it crossed my mind to look up the girls from the ship, maybe they could help me. That's if they were still at their last address.

I was desperate when we set out, I told Jack he had to be a good boy, hold my hand and not let go. He stared up at me with that big round face of his all smiles and trusting and it was all I could do not to cry. When things were blackest for me, all I ever wanted to do was rock him back and forth, trying to forget everything else.

Train tickets to Melbourne were more than £1, so I bought Jack a sandwich and myself a cup of tea, hoping to get lifts in lorries or cars. I wasn't thinking straight. In England, everywhere was closer, I've never got my head around distances here. We were lucky a few times with lifts, though there were long walks between. Then late in the afternoon, Jack started to grizzle and turn it on because he was hungry and I realised he hadn't eaten since breakfast, so I told him I'd find him something, soon as we stopped. But when that couple dropped us off, I knew I wasn't going to find any food out there, with no shops and it getting dark and even if I managed to cadge something from somewhere in return for washing up maybe, there'd be another meal after that and another, then what?

It was when the woman asked where we were headed that I realised how far we still had to go. I muttered something about finding another lift soon and once they'd gone, we started walking again, me holding Jack's hand, looking for a beach.

Dr Milson: Gradually, I've noticed a change come over her. Matron said she's been making herself useful and it seems to have done her good. She's less moody and isolated. So when she asked could she work in the garden, I had no objection. She can't escape, and being outdoors in the sun will do her good. Of course, I gave instructions she was not to have access to any sharp tools she could use to hurt herself, until we're more sure of her.

Head Gardener: I'm called head gardener but I'm the only one. The asylum can't afford any more men these days, but this was the first time I've had an offer of help from an inmate. To be honest, most are beyond it and besides, it can be heavy work and mostly boring. Digging up potatoes and suchlike. Pulling turnips, cutting cabbages. But she took to it willingly and proved a good worker. Then after a few weeks, she asked could we please plant some flowers. Pumpkins and turnips were all very well to feed inmates, she said, but there was nothing bright and cheerful to look at and wasn't that important? So I give it some thought and next time I came to work, I gave her some seeds for daisies and pansies that brought a smile to her face.

'Pansies,' she said, 'they were Jack's favourites! He pretended they were little people in fancy hats. I told him where I came from the old people called them Heartease, or Cuddle Me, but the best name of all was Jack-jump-up-and-kiss-me! Then I'd grab and hug him and we'd roll over on the floor, laughing.' She looked away for a minute and next thing she's down on her knees, starting to plant them round the edges of beds that faced the hospital.

She was a nice enough woman. Hard to imagine she'd done what she had. She seemed so kind. We were in the grounds one day, when some of the bigger inmates took a set against one patient who was barely five foot tall and you should have seen Bryant! She's not tall herself, but she stepped in and gave those women what for, defending Jilly, and from then on, the two of them were always together. Jilly looked up to Bryant like an older sister, even though she's in her fifties, so older.

Matron Baxter: When Bryant was being considered for release, I worried at the effect it might have on Jilly. What would she do without Bryant to protect her? She's been here since she was ten, having run away from her convent boarding school, when her family decided she was too rebellious for them to control. She won't be let out any time soon, if at all, which is a pity. She's been through such a lot. Uncontrollable when she first came, she'd break windows trying to get out, and we had to straightjacket her. She had constant bruises from being restrained but since she's had ECT, and more recently been operated on, she's as quiet as a little child, which is why the others pick on her, of course.

Bryant: There were times soon after I came that I'd think of Reg in a straightjacket, trussed up like a chook, unable to move. Tight enough to cramp his style, stop him getting his slimy arms round me. Or anyone else. I even wondered if he'd read about me in the papers. What I'd done? How he might have felt when he realised I'd murdered his only son? I hope if he did, he's sorry.

But before long, I barely gave him a thought. It was Jack I remembered. How I believed we neither of us had a future.

Dr Milson: So Kate – I assume I can call you Kate now you're almost due for release – have you thought any more about going back to England? To your family?

Kate: No. How can I? It would take me years to save the money and besides, I haven't written since I found out I was pregnant.

Dr Milson: Why not?

Kate: What would I say? Dear Mum, I had this child, your grandson, but I drowned him, so they sent me to an asylum, where I've been ever since. The weather remains warm, hoping this finds you well, your loving daughter, Kate.

Dr Milson: Yes, I can see it would be difficult. But surely, they must wonder what's happened to you?

Kate: Of course, but I'm not about to tell them.

Dr Milson: Never mind. We'll make sure you have a job to go to and somewhere to stay when you leave here.

Head Gardener: The last time she worked in the garden, I gave her a little packet of seeds to take with her, telling her to keep them in a dry, dark place and only plant them when she felt the time was right. In memory of her boy. She was a mite tearful at first, then she gave me a hug, which I hope Matron didn't see from her window, or it'd look like I'd been over-friendly with the inmates and I'd be in for it. That was the last I saw of her.

Matron Baxter: When she came into my office to say goodbye, I said, 'Well now, Bryant, has it really been ten years? It doesn't seem that long, does it?'

'Twice as long as my Jack's life. He would have been fifteen by now.' Then she said, 'I've said goodbye to Jilly, but I'm not sure she understood it's for good. So I've asked the gardener to keep an eye on her to make sure the others don't bully her. And I've made this. Would you please see she gets it after I've gone?'

She handed me a rag doll she'd made, the size of a human baby, and quite lifelike, with a smiling little face and dressed in pretty, handmade clothes.

'Why, that's lovely, Bryant.'

'It's from scraps in the sewing room, working in my spare time. But tell her it's from me, that it's to bring her luck. She's always wanted a baby of her own.'

Kate: When I came out, it was 1941 and we were at war again and it crossed my mind that perhaps my release had less to do with not being a danger to myself or others, but more to do with the war effort. That maybe Dr Milson thought I could make myself useful again, not in munitions, but in a hospital, where he thought I'd feel safe after living in one for ten years. If the new matron knew where I'd been, she didn't say, but merely asked what I could do. 'Home duties,' I told her. It sounded better than housekeeper, which I wasn't, and better than cleaner, which I was.

Australian Electoral Rolls –1943 Randwick: – Prince of Wales Hospital – home duties.

The hospital had been taken over by the army after the last war and re-named Fourth Australian Repatriation Hospital. Apart from a couple of big old stone buildings at the top of the site, it was nearly all Nissen huts, boiling in summer, freezing in winter, with twenty-five beds in each and a nurse in charge. I was only there to dust and mop floors, collect dirty linen, scour bedpans. I wasn't expected to talk to the patients. It was not my business to, I was told, but going through the huts each day brought the last war back to me. These were this war's Harolds, and if they spoke, I answered. Why would I deny them a bit of human company if that's what they wanted? They were a sad lot; maimed and blind, those on crutches waiting for limbs, some with their heads bandaged and those with half their faces blown away.

I lived in one of the huts at the back of the hospital with other cleaners and workers and when I first arrived the strangest thing was seeing myself in a mirror again after so many years. There were no mirrors at the asylum, or in Long Bay, so the last time I'd seen myself was in Glebe and the face that stared back at me I hardly knew. Far more lined, the hair greying and, where once it was short and cropped, now drawn back in a bun. There was a small mirror above the basin in our hut and I'd find myself sneaking a look whenever I passed as if I needed to make friends with this strange new person.

Then one day, the head cleaner and I were having a cup of tea in our break and she told me the hospital wasn't always for sick people, that it had started life as an orphanage, the Asylum for Destitute Children. As soon as I heard that, a chill come over me, like a bucket of iced water.

Head Cleaner: It was the nineteenth century, but still a terrible name for it. All those poor little mites left abandoned on streets, or dumped in here because their parents couldn't feed them. They had as many as eight hundred at a time, and there were deaths, of course. The usual measles and whooping cough, but others more suspicious, beatings, covered up. There's a cemetery behind the old buildings, with a few headstones still, you should go and look at it.

Kate: So I did, as soon as I had time to myself. It was overgrown, a few weathered headstones, mostly broken or fallen, the lettering hard to make out. But one, for a Francis Martin, aged three, died 18 October 1863, had me in tears. I'd always hated the idea of orphanages, maybe it harked back to Dad's fear of the workhouse, but this one had done better by little Francis than I had by Jack who would never have a head-stone and it was my fault.

Thankfully, no one at the hospital knew what I'd done, even though I hadn't changed my name. But with no photograph of me in the papers at the time, no one seemed to remember. Ten years is a long time in a life.

Then, one day the head cleaner showed me a newspaper she was reading, with the headline:

SIX DROWNED IN CREEK: MOTHER ENDS OWN AND
CHILDREN'S LIVES. Deniliquin, Sunday.

> Who'll Be Chief Mourner?
> I, said the Dove,
> I mourn for my love,
> I'll be Chief Mourner.

Head Cleaner: Can you believe it? And it's not as if she's alone. She's got a husband who cuts railway sleepers. And at twenty-nine she must have known what she was doing.

Kate: Maybe…

All I could think of was how this woman had succeeded where I'd failed.

Head Cleaner: It says she was being treated for nervous strain and worry, but all five? There were a hundred people out searching till they finally found the pram from the tyre tracks. She'd left it on the bridge over the creek with a note inside.

Kate: How old were the children?

Head Cleaner: The oldest was twelve, then eight, five, four and three months. They found the little ones first. It's a terrible, terrible thing. How could a mother do such a thing?

Kate: I said nothing, but from then on, I was scared I might give myself away or she'd find out somehow, so I planned to move on as soon as I could.

But before that could happen, I took the packet of seeds the head gardener had given me up to the little cemetery and planted them. For Jack, for Francis Martin and for each of those five children. The last seeds I planted for their mother, because I felt I knew her. I too, had been there.

Australian Electoral Rolls – 1949 Waterloo: Royal South Sydney Hospital, Joynton Avenue, Waterloo – hospital cleaner.

With no proper training – munitions didn't count – I stuck to cleaning. The army had made it clear once the war ended it would only want its own people working there so I began looking for another hospital, smaller and further away and moved there in '45.

Royal South Sydney was a public hospital where no one would know me or find out that I'd been locked away for years. The matron was a friendly enough woman who asked what else I could do, since they were short staffed. So I told her sewing and soon they had me making up towels and sheets, pillowcases, hospital gowns even. And when there was no sewing that needed doing, they put me in the office learning how to file and type. Only two fingers at first, but enough for envelopes and for the first time in years, I felt I was doing something more worthwhile, so I stayed there for five years.

Australian Electoral Rolls – 1954 – 15 Grosvenor Crescent, Summer Hill – hospital worker.

Kate: By now I had a little put by and was feeling more confident being out in the world. So I left the hospital and took a room in a boarding house in Summer Hill, an old terrace, a bit run-down, but the rooms were clean and comfortable, and it was close enough for me to walk to my new job.

Unlike other hospitals, Renwick was for infants under two whose parents couldn't afford doctors. The beds were cots and the walls painted primrose yellow, so it didn't feel like a hospital and the wards, twelve of them, had glass walls between, so light flowed through, making it a cheerful place to work

All this time, I'd managed to keep my past to myself. When they asked if I liked children, I said yes, that I'd had a son once, but he'd died, and they must have thought, having been a mother, I'd be good with children. I wasn't nursing them of course, only working in the office, where they gave me the title 'hospital worker'. General dogsbody more like. I fetched and carried, delivered messages to the wards, filed, typed (I was getting better and could manage business letters now) and generally worked hard, but I loved it. Occasionally when the nurses were busy, I even read to the children and every now and then there'd be some little boy who reminded me of Jack.

Australian Electoral Rolls – 1958 – 15 Grosvenor Crescent, Summer Hill – hospital worker.

Kate: While I was there, I spent most of my spare time in the garden, planting pansies wherever I could, not only for Jack, but because children everywhere loved them.

I was there, in all, eight years and now sixty-two, and Jack, had he lived, would have been thirty-seven. Old enough to have been a father himself, and for me to be a grandmother. Every time a grandmother came to the hospital to see some little mite in his cot, I'd think of what I'd done, and what I'd lost. And it had me wondering about my own parents. Pa and Ma were most probably dead, and I had no way of knowing where Lily was, assuming she and William had married and moved out. Perhaps I should have written when I came out of the asylum and confessed but, Pa would have been in his eighties and the shock might have killed him.

Australian Electoral Rolls – 1963 – Holt Homes, Acacia Road, Sutherland, hospital assistant.

Probably because I was getting older and thinking of Ma and Pa I decided to move from Renwick, away from small children, and take work in a nursing home for the elderly, as hospital assistant, meaning I'd do anything and everything. Answering phones in the office, doing jobs for matron or the nurses and, in my spare time, still planting flowers, which had become my hobby. But why should pansies be only for children, when they could brighten the lives of old people as well? So I planted some in memory of Pa and Ma, and since many residents were too frail or bedridden to make it into the gardens to see them up close, I asked Matron could I plant them in window boxes as well and she was delighted. She found money for seeds and I went from room to room, box to box, bringing little splashes of colour into their lives, all the while hoping Lily, or others, might have done as much for Ma and Pa.

I had little to do with the residents themselves, other than to say hello as I passed and mention the weather, always the weather, they liked that, but one day I saw a name I never expected to see again and thought, it can't be. Then I remembered he'd lived down this way. I never knew where exactly, but southern suburbs somewhere.

I checked and it was definitely his name on the door, and I could see his wife sitting beside him, holding his hand, but it was clear he no longer knew who she was. Then when she'd gone I slipped in, closed the door behind me and stood for some time staring down at his pathetic little form, white-haired and shrivelled under the covers and for an instant, it occurred to me it would be so simple to pick up a pillow and hold it to his face, wait till his arms stopped flailing, his twitching subsided. They'd most likely think he'd died in his sleep. But I couldn't. I felt no hate, no anger, nothing.

'Goodbye, Reg,' was all I said, and as I left the room, two women approached, his daughters, both women now in their forties, one with his red hair and I thought, 'What would you say if I told you you'd a half-brother, once?' But I didn't. After all, they'd done nothing to me.

Australian Electoral Rolls – 1980 – 1 Acacia Road, Sutherland – assistant.

Kate: I've been retired now some years, but still live here in staff quarters. I've nowhere else to go. I keep busy – better to wear away than rust away, as Ma would say. I sew and knit, children's clothes mostly, and toys they sell at their fetes, but I don't garden any more, too hard on the knees.

I still think of Jack, barely a day goes by when I don't, that I shouldn't have done what I did, but the sea swallows and the sea rejects. We don't decide. A creek is more certain.

The other day, Matron asked if I had any instructions for my funeral and I told her, no, but I've given her some money, enough to have me interred in an unmarked grave in Wollongong Cemetery and, if there's anything left over, maybe buy some pansies for the flower beds.

Lennie Duff: It's hard to believe I'm almost old enough for the pension when it doesn't seem all that long ago I turned fifty. We had the family over, our four, plus the six grandchildren, all underfoot and toys everywhere. The noise was unbelievable, but we love them and wouldn't have it any other way.

But every now and then, I look at the middle one, Billy, who's five, and it takes me back all those years to that Saturday morning on Brighton Beach and that little kid with his big head and damp, red curls tied to his mum inside her coat.

Dedicated to Jack Beeby, aged five, who drowned 8 May 1931 on Brighton Beach and is buried in Wollongong Cemetery.